EMBEZZLEMENT LEADS TO . . .

"I'm going to die," she thought.

The axles teetered sickeningly along the edge of the bridge, as if in slow motion. She knew the car was about to fall. Could she bear the jolt when the metal hit the water? What if the convertible flipped upside down in the air? A surge of panic blurred the questions. Before her mind could sort out the answers she had scrambled onto the seat and jumped. She felt herself hurtling away from the car—down, down, into the dark, blue waters of Mission Bay.

. . . MISSION BAY MURDER

MISSION BAY MURDER

PHILIP CARLTON WILLIAMS

PaperJacks LTD.

TORONTO   NEW YORK

AN ORIGINAL

PaperJacks

MISSION BAY MURDER

PaperJacks LTD.

330 STEELCASE RD. E., MARKHAM, ONT. L3R 2M1
210 FIFTH AVE., NEW YORK, N.Y. 10010

First edition published July 1988

This is a work of fiction in its entirety. Any resemblance to actual people, places or events is purely coincidental.

This original PaperJacks edition is printed from brand-new plates made from newly set, clear, easy-to-read type. No part of this book may be reproduced or transmitted in any form or by any means, electronic or mechanical, including photography, recording, or any information storage or retrieval system, without permission in writing from the publisher.

10 9 8 7 6 5 4 3 2 1

ISBN 0-7701-0953-5
Copyright © 1988 by Philip Carlton Williams
All rights reserved.
Printed in the USA

To Boots, with love.

Chapter I

Sheila Simmons felt her high heel snap as she mashed the brake pedal to the floorboard. Her red-orange hair whipped behind her in the open Fiat Spider convertible. Her blue eyes were white with horror.

"He's trying to kill me!" She forced the thought from her mind as she lifted her foot from the brake and jammed the accelerator, trying to outmaneuver the black Porsche. The speedometer jumped forward—fifty, sixty, seventy—as she approached the high-arching bridge.

She could not see his face behind the tinted windows, but there was no mistaking his message. He was on her right side now, swerving toward her, crunching metal against metal, forcing her into the oncoming lanes. She slammed the brakes again, the screech of the tires overpowering the roaring motor.

He swerved again, this time with all the fury of the Porsche. Her tiny Fiat was no match. She felt the steering wheel jerk to the left, straight for the opposite railing. She stood on the brakes with all her weight. There was no time to consider the traffic. The railing was too close. And now it was just in front of the hood.

"It won't hold me!" she thought.

It was a wooden retaining wall. The bridge was under construction.

"God, make me stop!"

The fender snapped easily through the plywood panel. The hood was dangling in empty space.

It was that damned letter that started everything. Sent Previt after Sheila's Fiat and had the cops thinking I murdered her. I knew I shouldn't have looked at it.

It was stuck to the back of a memorandum. Some turkey in Previt's office must have been eating glazed doughnuts or something. It was stamped "CONFIDENTIAL," which in corporation language means "Don't look at this unless your name is on it." But I'm a lawyer. So to me, "CONFIDENTIAL" means "Take a good, long look. You might not see this sucker again."

I had been house counsel for Argotech Enterprises for two years, and you'd think that would mean something, but not at Argotech. I was the last one to know what was going on around that place. All I knew was that we were designing some heavy-duty weapons for the navy. Even though I drafted the contracts for every weapon, the pictures and blueprints were always kept in sealed envelopes in a locked file. So when the confidential letter came across my desk by mistake, I jumped at the chance to read it, figuring I could learn something about the things we were making and then send the letter on with no one the wiser. But that's not what happened.

The top page wasn't confidential at all. It was a memo to me from Bob Goren, Argotech's president, thanking me for the work I did on the Hypercorp deal, the biggest contract Argotech had ever signed. The sticky second page had nothing to do with the first page. It was an original, signed letter:

CONFIDENTIAL   CONFIDENTIAL

ARGOTECH ENTERPRISES
5500 Sorrento Valley Road
Del Mar, California
January 17, 1987

Mr. James Terrell, President
Gopher, Inc.
4027 Crown Point Drive #524
San Diego, California

Dear Mr. Terrell:

This letter will confirm our understanding whereby Gopher, Inc., will perform consulting services for Argotech Enterprises during calendar year 1987. Gopher will be paid $250,000 per month in the form of a check mailed to your principal place of business, the first such check to be delivered to you on or about May 31, 1987.

> Sincerely,
> Charles T. Previt
> Senior Vice President
> and Chief Financial Officer

The letter wasn't as juicy as I had hoped, but it was plenty weird. For example, it said nothing about the quality or duration of Gopher's consulting services. What if Gopher screwed us over? How would we cancel the arrangement? And furthermore, I had never heard of any consulting firm named Gopher, Inc. Why would an unknown firm be worth a quarter of a million dollars a month? That came to three million dollars a year. Argotech's operating profit in 1986 was only four and a half million dollars, and here Previt was arranging for this Gopher company to gobble up two-thirds of that in 1987.

But what really got me was the bold signature: Charles T. Previt. He was the man who had hired me. It should have occurred to me during the job interview that he was a little, ah, unbalanced. Unbalanced enough to kill people. He kept me waiting forty-five minutes while I sat outside his office, feeling stupid in front of Lisa, his secretary.

Just when I had given up on the interview, Previt made his grand entrance. He was fortyish, with slick black hair and a Clark Gable mustache. The way he strutted you could almost hear the drumroll and the trumpets. When I stood up to greet him he shook my right hand like a county politician.

"Mike, Mike, I'm so glad you're still here. I'm terribly sorry you had to wait so long." His concerned blue eyes showed all the sincerity of a water moccasin, but for some reason I ate it up.

"It's okay," I responded in my southern drawl. "Lisa is a mighty fine hostess." Previt's secretary smiled shyly, but didn't look up from her typing.

"Yes, we plan to keep her," Previt laughed. "Come on in. We have some business to discuss."

Previt was one of those salesmen who could talk a dog off a meat wagon. He gave me this speech about how defense contractors were always in trouble with the press because they didn't listen to their lawyers. I got the feeling I would be an important player at Argotech, sought out by all the bigwigs for advice on sensitive issues. Before I had opened my mouth he offered me fifty thousand dollars a year to serve as Argotech's house counsel. He didn't even notice my white socks.

"I'm going to die," she thought.

The axles teetered sickeningly along the edge of the bridge, as if in slow motion. She knew the car was about to fall. Could she bear the jolt when the metal hit the water? What if the convertible flipped upside down in the air? A surge of panic blurred the questions. Before her mind could sort out the answers she had scrambled onto the seat and jumped. She felt herself hurtling away from the car—down, down, into the dark, blue waters of Mission Bay.

The black Porsche sped safely down the bridge, turning eastward when it reached Sea World Drive.

I went straight home and called all my friends back in Ocracoke. Here I'd just graduated from Blue Ridge School of Law with grades that put me near the bottom of my class and I'd be making more money than old Judge Battle back home. Don't get the wrong idea. I could've made better grades if I had set my mind to it. I just never did care much about law school. Even Dad wanted me to fish scallops like my two brothers.

After a few months I figured out that my position was damned petty and not the least bit sensitive. I wasn't too thrilled about the way Previt was handling my paycheck, either. Lisa whispered to me one day that he was fudging my salary into the Hypercorp contract and that Hypercorp would probably be passing it on to the government.

If I hadn't been so starry-eyed during the job interview, I would have known something was fishy. Even after six months on the job I was too proud to admit to myself that Previt had hired me just to pad Argotech's expense budget. Hypercorp was paying us on a cost-plus-20% arrangement. That meant that if Argotech could prove it had a million dollars in costs, Hypercorp would have to pay us that million plus a two-hundred-thousand-dollar bonus. But if Previt could inflate those costs to two million dollars, the bonus would rise to four hundred thousand. So he went out and found some innocent-looking expenses, like my salary for instance, to jack up the budget. Then he realized he couldn't hire somebody who would ask questions. So he found an unsophisticated bumpkin—me—and he must have been salivating.

You'd think after I got wise I'd have the good sense to find another job. Not me. I was thinking, "What the hell? The money's good, I like my co-workers, and I'm out here in southern California." I let two years pass before I started worrying about what would happen to me if Previt got caught. Then Lisa started telling me stuff about Previt—how much money he was making off the company. And the more I thought about it, the more I worried. By the time the letter came across my desk I was more nervous than a whore in church.

The Fiat groaned and fell, the hood turning slowly forward as the car accelerated toward the water. Everything was upside down when it hit the surface with a loud smack. A white fountain sprayed upward like smoke from a bomb.

Nearby, the fishermen in Ned Sargent's rowboat were spellbound. All four tires could be seen bobbing among the whitecaps. Then two big bubbles broke along either side of the car. Two wheels vanished, then four.

Ned's hands were shaking.

"God help whoever was driving that car."

The letter had my mind spinning. I took the Coast Highway home so I could park along the shore and think awhile. I knew a spot that reminded me of my hometown on the outer banks of North Carolina. When I was little I used to coast my bicycle faster and faster down the sand dunes until the breeze whipped my hair back straight and made my eyes water. Then I would always forget whatever problems were bothering me. But today the fresh wind off the breakers didn't clear my head. I was still lost in thought when I left the view and drove home to Solana Beach.

It was starting to get dark as I parked my new Buick in the carport and walked around to the sidewalk. I clumped absently up the wooden steps to my condo entrance, unlocked the door, and stepped inside. Something hit me on the back of my neck.

"Dammit, Spike!" I yelled. I swatted the cat off my shoulder and watched her scamper into the kitchen.

Spike's a female calico. She got her name by spiking holes in my thumb with her teeth. I've called her a few other names, but Spike's the one that stuck. A few days after I bought her at the Humane Society she learned to claw her way to the top of the doorframe like a tree monkey. I never saw anything like it, so I showed all my friends. They just thought it was great. Couldn't believe it. But after months of being greeted by a kitten jumping on my neck, I got tired of it. Problem was I couldn't figure out how to make her stop. Once I tried reaching up to grab her before I walked through the door, and she bit my thumb.

I sat on the sofa and pulled the letter from my jacket. What was Previt up to this time? I knew my curiosity wouldn't be satisfied until I checked out Gopher, Inc., with my own eyes.

It was Ned's six-year-old son who first saw the red-orange tangle, like a clump of seaweed bobbing in the water thirty feet away.

"Dad, look! What is it?"

Ned Sargent knew what it was even before he saw the green blouse beneath the hair.

"It's a woman," he answered numbly.

Chapter II

The Friday morning sun smiled down at me because I was playing hooky from work. I chose a scenic detour through Mission Bay Park, past the bay beaches with names like Vacation Village, Fiesta Island, and Inspiration Point. Sailboats were everywhere, like a thousand dancing kites set free to float upon the waves. I drove across the old concrete bridge and turned right onto Crown Point Drive, the lazy boulevard separating the well-manicured lawns on my left from the water on my right. Across the bay was the skyline of San Diego; but I was not interested in the view. I was focusing on the house numbers: 2032, 2046. . . . 4027 would be a mile or two down the street.

As I approached the end of Crown Point Drive the road narrowed and the view changed from bay to tidal marsh. There was a sign in front of the high-rise apartment building: 4027 Crown Point Drive. I parked near the front entrance and walked up to the security door. Buzzer buttons were arranged next to the names of the residents. I pulled the letter from my coat pocket and found the apartment number: 524. I scanned down the list of names until I found the number. There it was: 524—J. Terrell.

It took a second for the information to sink in. I hadn't expected an apartment. At the very least I expected a small business office. So now I had a choice: I could go home and forget the whole thing, or I could press the button. A smart lawyer would have gone home. I pressed the button and heard a crackle from the speaker. No response. I waited. After more than a minute I pressed the button again. More static, then silence.

As I turned to leave, a U.S. Postal Service jeep pulled up to the building. A middle-aged mail carrier hopped out and walked to the rear of the jeep. I had an idea.

"Excuse me! . . . Sir! . . ," I began the charade. "I'm on my way out. Anything for James Terrell in five twenty-four?"

He picked up a stack of mail from the jeep and thumbed through the letters. "Let's see. I don't remember anything for Terrell. You're new here, right?"

I nodded.

"Nope. Nothing here, unless you want these coupons for Occupant. We're supposed to put these in every box."

"No thanks."

I shook my head and trotted down the steps to my car.

I drove west toward the ocean and found the business district of Pacific Beach, one of San Diego's coastal neighborhoods. There was a pay phone outside a liquor store on Garnet Avenue. I lifted the receiver and dialed information.

"Directory assistance, what city please?"

"San Diego."

"Go ahead, please."

"James Terrell. T-E-R-R-E-L-L."

I heard the operator clicking buttons in the background, which meant the name was not showing up on the computer screen.

"I have no listing for a James Terrell. I have a Mark Terrell on Fay Avenue in La Jolla."

"No. I'm sure it's James Terrell on Crown Point Drive. Maybe it's a new listing."

Again a pause and more clicking.

"I'm not showing anyone by that name in San Diego."

"Okay. Thanks." I hung up the phone.

My investigation wasn't panning out the way I had hoped. Still, the fact that I had located an actual address with Terrell's name on it intrigued me. Was there really a consultant named James Terrell, or was the apartment just a mail drop? I reached for the telephone book and flipped the yellow pages until I reached the heading "INVESTIGATORS." An ad near the bottom of the page caught my attention:

PACIFIC BEACH INVESTIGATIONS
CORPORATE-CIVIL-LEGAL
SHEILA SIMMONS-STATE LICENSE
#AX90532
7 DAYS/24 HOURS

There was a Garnet Avenue address and a telephone number next to the ad. I dialed the number.

"Good afternoon, PBI." The female voice sounded pleasant enough.

"Yes. Ms. Sheila Simmons, please."

"I'm sorry, Sheila's on the other line. Maybe I can help you. I'm her assistant."

I hesitated. One thing being a corporate lawyer had taught me was to deal with the top dog whenever possible.

"I'm just down the street. Is Ms. Simmons available for an appointment this morning?"

"Oh, you don't need an appointment. Sheila's been looking for new business all week."

"I see." Again I hesitated. "Well, tell her I'm on my way up to see her. I'll be there in a few minutes."

I hung up the receiver. I felt half amused, half disappointed. The voice hadn't said, "Ms. Simmons." It had said, "Sheila." And even a hick lawyer knows you don't tell a stranger your company is looking for business.

What the hell, I rationalized. Could be a temporary receptionist. But I wasn't real confident I had found the right place.

The only sign of Pacific Beach Investigations on Garnet Avenue was a frosted-glass door bearing the white letters "PBI" inside the outline of a shield. Opening the door, I stepped into a dark corridor that led to a flight of narrow wooden steps. At the top of the steps was another glass door with the same "PBI" logo.

I felt good about the place. There were brick buildings like this one in my hometown. There were always little offices hidden upstairs: a law firm above the drugstore; a dental chair looking out over the five-and-dime; a notary public or CPA paying rent to the savings and loan.

The hollow sound of my footsteps echoed loudly against the corridor walls. The landing at the top of the stairway was unlit. I imagined a female version of Sam Spade waiting for me behind the glass door. I was not prepared for the scene that hit me.

The room inside was filled with a smoky haze creeping around the bare walls. Two redheads—one fat and one thin—were carrying on separate telephone conversations in voices much too loud. One of the women, the fat one, couldn't have been more than seventeen years old. She had a cute pug nose and bright blue eyes. But she was too heavy for the room's only seat, an aluminum picnic chair that wavered and bent as her blue-jeaned derriere jerked with every sweep of her fingers. The long ash of the cigarette that dangled from her moist lipstick moved in counterpoint to the rickety metal.

I gathered she was the girl to whom I had spoken. I could just make out a few of her words to the effect that "Sheila" would be "unable to investigate the case further until PBI receives some payment for the last three bills."

The other woman, who I assumed to be Sheila Simmons, had the long sensuous figure of a fashion model, accented with pumpkin-red hair. She was in her late twenties and wore jeans with a green sleeveless top. Her clothing clashed just enough with her hair to lend her an aura of working-class sexiness—a sort of "I-know-I-look-a-little-different-but-I'm-sharp-enough-to-pull-it-off" appearance.

She sat on the floor in the corner near the telephone jack. Her conversation had something to do with some photographs she needed on Monday. She was also smoking, and like the teenager, she waved her cigarette around as she spoke, as though the listener could see the imaginary illustrations in the air. She was leaning against the only other item of furniture in the room: a metal file cabinet.

My eyes were watering from the smoke as the chubby one ended her call. The flimsy chair squeaked ominously as she twisted her body to look up at me.

"You must be the guy who called a few minutes ago," she said, lowering her voice. Sheila Simmons was still trying to talk on the phone.

"That's right," I answered softly. "My name is Michael Thompson. Do you think Ms. Sim . . . uh . . . Sheila will be long?"

"I doubt it." She stood up to shake my hand, unaware that the seat cushion was partly stuck to her jeans. The chair rose with her a few inches then collapsed back against the floor with a loud crash as her cigarette tumbled across her white blouse.

"Sorry about that." She winced, looking nervously over at Sheila, whose face had turned white.

"I guess Sheila's going to have to buy some new furniture for this place," she continued, making no effort to retrieve the chair or wipe the ash from her chest. "I was just going to introduce myself. I'm Penny Boykins, Sheila's sister. I'm also her assistant."

She spoke proudly, holding out her hand.

"Where do the clients sit?" I asked, shaking her hand lightly.

"Sheila sets up meetings away from the office whenever she can."

Penny walked over to the file cabinet and pulled out a yellow legal pad.

"We might as well start your file while we're waiting for Sheila."

She handed me the pad and pen.

"Put your name, address, and phone number at the top of the page and we'll keep the file under your last name, unless you want us to use a different name." She sounded like a schoolgirl reciting a poem. "We charge thirty-five dollars an hour, plus expenses, but there usually aren't many expenses."

Sheila finished her conversation.

"I'm Sheila Simmons," she said, standing. "You'll have to forgive my office, or maybe I should say the lack of an office. I worked out of my home until August and we've never gotten around to furnishing this place." She held my attention as she spoke, her smile betrayed by a look of experienced sadness in her blue eyes. "Tell me how we can help you."

I stood awkwardly, glancing from Sheila to Penny, aware of my own sense of conflicting emotions: On the one hand, Sheila was an attractive woman and I needed an investigator right away. On the other hand, Sheila and Penny hardly seemed like the right team to investigate a complicated charge of embezzlement.

Without saying anything, I handed Sheila the letter. She looked it over briefly and copied the relevant names, dates, and addresses onto a small piece of paper that she then shoved into her purse. She started to hand the letter back to me, but Penny intercepted it quickly and looked it over herself while Sheila rolled her eyes.

"Little sister wants to learn the trade," she laughed. "I've told her it's a lousy profession, but she won't listen."

Penny looked up. "So who made you my mother?" she snapped defiantly.

I noted the family resemblance. Penny and Sheila shared many of the same facial features, but Penny's rested on the body of a cantaloupe.

Sheila sighed. "As I was saying, it's a lousy profession because there's so little interesting work right now, which is why you're particularly welcome, Mr. . . ."

"Thompson," I answered. "Call me Mike." Sheila was studying me.

"Well, Mike, it's almost lunchtime and we only have one chair in this office. Why don't we continue this discussion down the street at Pedro's? Do you like Mexican food?"

Pedro's was a popular Mexican restaurant, certain to be packed with tourists and beachgoers. It was famous not so much for its food as for its reputation as a San Diego singles bar "meat market."

"Is there someplace a bit less crowded?" I asked.

Penny piped up, "Take him to Nolan's. Don't you have any class?"

Sheila blushed and glared back at Penny.

"It's okay," I said. "I'm paying."

"Nolan's it is," said Sheila.

Penny handed me the letter.

"You guys go on," she piped. "Don't worry about me. Three's a crowd." She took the yellow pad from my hands, tore off the top sheet where I had written my name and address, and filed it in the cabinet.

Sheila led me to the door.

"Don't stay too late," Penny called after us. Sheila closed the office door behind us and marched down the old steps in front of me.

"I don't know what to do with her," she sighed, half to herself. "Five months on the job and she already knows everything. I guess if she didn't spend the day with me she'd be out getting pregnant."

The sun was unusually hot as we stepped out onto the street.

We entered the cocktail lounge at Nolan's. Four or five couples were talking quietly in dark booths along the walls. The central tables were empty. I was a little uneasy about the number of people within earshot of our conversation, especially when I wasn't too sure I was going to hire Sheila. But before I could suggest another restaurant, Sheila had already ordered a Scotch from the barmaid. I shrugged my shoulders and ordered a light beer. After the waitress had brought our drinks, Sheila began.

"So, tell me about the letter." She downed a hearty slug of the Scotch. "What's your relationship to Gopher?"

"Nothing at all," I said, taking a sip of the beer. "That's one of the problems. I'm Argotech's house counsel. I came across this letter by accident."

"And you suspect some funny business," Sheila interrupted.

"That's right. This one consulting agreement will eat up over half of Argotech's profits."

Sheila finished her Scotch in two more gulps.

"Sounds like your friend Mr. Previt has both hands in the cookie jar."

I squirmed a bit in my seat as I looked around the bar to see if anyone had heard her comment.

"The thought had occurred to me," I whispered. She studied my face silently for a few seconds.

"So why do you need a private investigator?" she asked finally.

I told her about my trip to Crown Point Drive.

"I need someone to watch the place. I want to find out if it's just a mail drop or if there really is a legitimate Gopher company. If the whole thing's a scam I'll need some rock-solid evidence to take to our internal auditors."

"Why not tell the police?"

"They wouldn't investigate this thing based on one letter. More likely they'd tell Previt I'd filed a complaint, and I'd lose my job. Everyone would believe Previt."

"So why do you trust the internal auditors? Couldn't Previt buy them off?"

She gestured to the waitress for another round of drinks.

"Internal auditors are a special breed. They get their kicks finding dirt on everybody."

"Careful." Sheila faked a hurt expression. "You're forgetting I'm also in the dirt-finding business."

I smiled awkwardly.

"No offense. What I meant was that no one would be stupid enough to offer money to an internal auditor. It would be like trying to bribe a nun. Anyway, I've got nothing to lose. All I plan to do is drop an anonymous note with some evidence in the auditors' mailbox and wait to see what happens."

"Sounds simple enough."

Sheila was well into her second drink.

The conversation turned to other subjects.

"Isn't Penny a little young for your line of work?" I asked.

"You mean for a sleazy operation like mine?"

"I didn't say that."

"You didn't have to. But don't worry. I feel the same way you do about it." She stirred the remnants of her drink, clinking the ice cubes around with her swizzle stick.

"At first I hired Penny to organize some files. Then she started begging me to take her out in the field. I figured she'd lose interest when she had to sit in a parked car for three hours waiting for some client's wife to walk out with another man. Instead she kept wanting to tag along."

"Maybe it runs in the family," I offered. Sheila was eyeing me pretty thoroughly.

"How'd you know that?" she asked.

"Know what?"

"My father's a detective," she said. "I was even married once to a cop. He wanted a doting housewife and lots of kids." She stared down at her empty glass. "You'd think I'd have learned something from my father. I guess a part of me was attracted to men like him—cops in uniform—but there was no way I was going to let some damn rookie cop own me. So now I'm an old maid with an apartment in La Jolla and it'll take more than one man to get me out of there."

I could tell the liquor was beginning to get to her. It was time to give her the bad news.

"Listen Sheila, I really think I have to look around before I hire anyone."

She looked hurt. "I talk too much, don't I?"

Her blue eyes became so sad that part of me wanted to reach across the table and stroke her hair. I had been away from home for two years, and I knew about loneliness. Instead, I just shook my head.

"No, you don't talk too much. It's just that this is an important case. If Previt finds out what I'm up to before I can pin a case on him, he'll have me fired and then sue me for defamation. One wrong step and I can kiss California goodbye."

Sheila grabbed my hand. "Give me one afternoon," she said. "If I don't impress you by tonight, you won't owe anything and you can hire somebody else."

I had trouble meeting her stare. Finally I surrendered.

"Okay," I said. "But a few hours is all I can give you. In the meantime I'll be considering other agencies."

"Fair enough." She gave my hand a playful slap and stood up to leave. "Why don't you come around to my place tonight after dinner. Say eight o'clock. I'll show you what I've dug up."

I suppose I should have been shocked at the invitation, but after viewing the scene in Sheila's office I was beginning to expect unorthodox behavior from her.

"Sure, why not?" I said, but I was already regretting my decision. What good could it do to send a half-drunk amateur out to work on my case?

By the time the waitress brought the check Sheila was out the door.

The sunset had left a patch of gray sky over the ocean when I parked on La Jolla Boulevard. Sheila's apartment was on the fourth floor of a modern building a few blocks from the beach. There was a security panel near the main entrance, similar to the one at the Crown Point address, only this time I had no problem getting an answer.

"Mike? Is that you?"

I recognized Sheila's voice.

"You guessed right," I said into the microphone. "You must be a private eye."

"Shut up and take the elevator," she laughed.

The door to her apartment was open a crack when I got there. I was about to knock when she opened it. There she stood in a bright red cocktail dress, her wavy hair flowing across her shoulders.

"Come on in," she said with a smile.

I stood dumbfounded as she waltzed inside to the sofa. She sat near one end, crossing her long legs with a gentle swish.

"Sit here next to me," she said, slapping the seat cushion. "You can see better."

I moved in slowly, feeling certain I was getting myself into some kind of trouble but not minding terribly much. I sat next to her and tried unsuccessfully to compose myself. In the soft light of the table lamp I could see she was a true redhead with clusters of brown freckles on her nose and cheekbones. The faint fragrance of perfume triggered a flurry of butterflies in my stomach.

"Take a look at these," she said. "I've been working all afternoon."

I noticed for the first time that there were a number of documents in her hand. The top sheet was a telex:

NO GOPHER, INC., FOUND IN SECRETARY
OF STATE'S INDEX OF CORPORATIONS
OR LIMITED PARTNERSHIPS. NO LISTING
UNDER GOPHER CORPORATION, GOPHER
COMPANY, GOPHER LTD., OR OTHER
SIMILAR VARIATIONS. NO LISTING
EITHER AS CALIFORNIA CORPORATION
OR AS OUT-OF-STATE CORPORATION
DOING BUSINESS HERE.

The second page was similar:

NO JAMES TERRELL FOUND IN SECRETARY
OF STATE'S INDEX OF PRINCIPALS. OTHER
TERRELLS INCLUDE WILLIAM (2) AND
JOHN, ALL OUT OF STATE.

I looked up.
"Keep reading," Sheila said.
I turned to the third page. It was a government form from the San Diego County Department of Business Licenses. "GOPHER, INC., RESERVED BY SHEILA SIMMONS" was printed near the top of the page. Sheila's address and signature followed.
"What's this one mean?" I asked.
Sheila clucked disapprovingly.
"I thought all corporate lawyers knew how to read these things," she said. "It states very clearly that I have reserved the business name Gopher, Inc., in San Diego County."
I shrugged my shoulders.
"Congratulations," I said, not yet appreciating

the cleverness of her maneuver. "Now you have a business name worthy of your office."

Sheila gave me a playful push.

"Wrong, airhead," she laughed. "I reserved the name to prove a point. If the county was willing to reserve the name for me, that means no one else has asked for it."

"Like Previt, for instance?"

"Exactly."

"So why'd you pay fifty bucks to reserve it yourself? Couldn't you just ask them if the name was available?"

Sheila stood up and posed happily in front of me, holding one hand behind her head like a fashion model.

"Here's where I impress you," she said, patting me on the head. "By reserving the name myself I guaranteed that the county will contact me if Previt tries to register the company."

She curtsied and sat down again. There was an innocent magic about her that reminded me of Shirley Temple, only it radiated from the body of Raquel Welch. I found myself staring at her in admiration.

"Well, aren't you going to finish reading?" she said coyly, deflecting my gaze back to the remaining pages.

"What are these?" I asked.

There were at least a dozen government forms of all shapes and sizes.

"More of the same," she said, standing up again. I watched her walk toward the kitchen. "No listing of Gopher, Inc., or James Terrell in any state or local agency I could think of. Hey, you want something to drink? I bought some light beer for you."

"Sure. Why not," I called back.

I heard her open the refrigerator door. She reappeared a few seconds later holding a mug in one hand and a mixed drink in the other. She handed me the beer and plopped down next to me again.

"Besides all the paperwork, I did some investigating on my own," she said. "I called some friends of mine in the navy and the telephone company."

She flashed me another pose, as if to say, "Aren't you impressed?"

"And what did you find out?" I asked as coolly as I could. I didn't want her to know quite yet that she had already won the job.

"Well," she began. "My navy friend works in the contract department. He's never heard of Gopher, Inc., or James Terrell."

"And your telephone friend?"

"He checked the Crown Point apartment in the reverse directory and the unlisted index. No Gophers, no Terrells."

I scratched my head, trying to add up all the pieces.

"You mean the apartment's just a phony mail drop?"

"Bingo," she said, pointing her glass at my nose. "I can try a few more contacts Monday, but I think we've got the picture. Besides, you haven't hired me yet."

She put her drink down on the coffee table and

folded her hands in her lap. I was torn between telling her she was hired and planting a big kiss on her mouth.

"Okay," I said, suppressing a smile.

She threw her arms around me.

"Oh, Michael, how exciting!" she cried. "I'll get right to work first thing tomorrow."

She jumped up and ran to the front door.

"Call me Sunday afternoon." she said, giggling. "This is going to be so much fun!"

Her sudden change of attitude caught me off guard. She whisked me out the door totally bewildered. But something in her eyes told me I might be more than just a client. I wandered down the hall, forgetting that I was still holding the beer mug. I carried it all the way to my car.

Sheila's spell stayed with me as I drove home with the empty mug. I had no way of knowing that the next time I would hear her name would be from the mouth of a homicide detective.

Chapter III

You'd think with all the depressing stuff going on at work I'd have found a happy way to spend my Sundays. Instead, I was a San Diego Padres fan. It was only two weeks into the season and they were already hopelessly mired in last place. To make matters worse they were losing ten to nothing in Shea Stadium, and I was about to finish off my third can of Miller Lite. Spike was asleep next to my socks.

I grabbed the telephone from the coffee table and dialed Sheila's number. The phone rang only once. I was surprised when a male voice answered.

"Uh . . . maybe I've got the wrong number. I was trying to reach Pacific Beach Investigations."

"You got the right number," the voice answered gruffly. "What's your name?"

"My name ain't none of your business unless you work for Sheila Simmons," I snapped. Beer makes me cranky.

I heard the man take a deep breath.

"Well, buddy"—he coughed—"you're gonna have to find another private investigator. Sheila Simmons was killed in a car wreck yesterday afternoon."

I dropped the telephone, startling Spike, who scampered into the kitchen. By the time I lifted the receiver again, the line was dead. I collected myself enough to dial the number. The same voice answered.

"Hello," I said. "I called just a few seconds ago. What happened to Sheila?"

My heart was racing.

"You never told me your name." I didn't like the man's tone of voice.

"Michael Thompson," I said, "What's yours?"

The man puffed noisily.

"Listen up, buddy, I'm a police detective. So far, what we have is a red Fiat Spider at the bottom of Mission Bay and a witness who says you were the last one to visit Sheila before she was killed. So you can come down here and talk to us or we can go up there and arrest you. Take your pick."

"Okay, I can take a hint," I responded. "Give me a hour."

"Be here at five-thirty or we come looking."

The man hung up the receiver. I felt numb all over.

The black Porsche was parked near the front steps of the mansion. In the library, two men were talking. The older man poured the champagne, offering one of the glasses to the man with the dark mustache.

"Well done," he said, lifting his glass to toast the younger man.

"We still have Thompson to worry about." The dark-haired man did not lift his glass.

"He should be easier than the woman," the older man said, smiling.

"Yeah, but he has the letter."

The older man nodded sadly.

"You should never have let it out of your sight. But that is all water over the dam. I'm sure we can find a way to persuade him to give it back."

The younger man finally lifted his champagne.

"We won't need to if I find it first."

The older man clinked the glass and smiled.

I found Spike hiding behind the refrigerator. I clutched her against my chest and walked outside. The *San Diego Tribune* was at my feet on the porch. The afternoon sunlight glittered on the dry leaves lining the walkway. I carried the newspaper inside and dropped Spike on the carpet by the sofa. I found the article I was looking for in the local section:

MISSION BAY CRASH
KILLS PACIFIC BEACH
INVESTIGATOR

Sheila Simmons, 31, investigator for Pacific Beach Investigations, a local private investigation firm, was apparently killed yesterday afternoon when her small sports car crashed through a bridge railing on Ingraham Street Bridge near Sea World. Although no witnesses could be reached for comment, police sources indicated Ms. Simmons was traveling southbound on Ingraham Street at a high rate of speed when she lost control of her car, which crossed over two northbound lanes and crashed over the bridge railing into Mission Bay. Due to the record tides yesterday afternoon, police were not confident Ms. Simmons's body would be located quickly, but indicated that tides should return to near normal today. Ms. Simmons is survived by her father, Joseph Boykins of Ocean Beach, and her sister Penny Boykins, also of Ocean Beach.

That was it. The death of Sheila Simmons. Maybe it was the coldness of the news article that sent me back to San Diego, or maybe it was the detective's tone of voice. The only thing I was sure of was that too many strange things were happening to me and none of them made any sense. I decided to bring Spike along with me on the trip. Somehow, the shock of Sheila's death made Spike seem more important to me.

After I had parked my Buick near Sheila's office, I placed Spike in the back seat in an open cardboard box I had filled with fresh kitty litter. I cracked the windows just enough so she couldn't crawl out, and then locked her in and headed up to Sheila's office.

The sound of my footsteps on the stairway was unsettling, more hollow than before. I felt the same sense of déjà vu I had experienced the last time I climbed those steps, but this time the mood was eerie—not pleasant at all. I had once been on a similar staircase after the death of a friend.

I was remembering Mary-Louise. She had been our baby-sitter when I was five years old and my younger sister was only three. She would sing to us with her ukulele and teach us funny songs. She must have been about sixteen years old at the time. Her boyfriend had come by with his motorcycle to pick her up when my parents got home from dinner.

Later that night, while we were getting ready for bed, the telephone rang. Dad told us that Mary-Louise had been killed when the motorcycle struck a passing car. We didn't know much about motorcycles but we started crying when we understood that Mary-Louise would never be coming back. I remember starting to go upstairs to my bedroom and noticing that Mary-Louise had left her ukulele near the bottom of the steps.

The office door was open at the top of the stairway. Just inside, I could see a young policeman in uniform talking to a grey-haired man wearing a sportcoat and tie. They both turned toward me as I neared the office.

"You must be Thompson," the older one said as I entered. "Thanks for coming down."

I recognized the gravelly voice from our telephone conversation earlier, but the man's attitude had improved.

"What can I do for you gentlemen?" I asked, trying to mask my nervousness. It would have been more comfortable to be sitting down, but there were no safe chairs in Sheila's office.

"You can start by telling us where you were Friday night," said the younger one.

I described some of my conversation with Sheila without getting into details about James Terrell and Gopher, Inc. I could feel the beer swimming around in my head.

"Listen, guys," I concluded. "The way I understand it, Sheila's car went through a bridge railing yesterday afternoon. Does it make sense that I would go to her apartment on Friday night, leave without her, and then fix her car so it would drive off a bridge on Saturday afternoon?" Neither man could appreciate my logic.

"Trouble is," said the younger cop, "we think someone forced her off the bridge. And there's no doubt the incident happened on Saturday, the day after you saw her twice." The light from the far window highlighted the lines of his face. He was slightly older than me. Maybe late thirties.

"How can you tell someone forced her off the bridge?" I asked.

The older cop broke in.

"We'll ask the questions," he said. "Where did you go Friday night after you left the deceased." The police vocabulary, with words like "incident" and "deceased," annoyed me. It was only a matter of time before they called me a "suspected perpetrator."

"I drove home. No stops. No witnesses."

The older cop was glaring at me. "Anyone see you come home?"

I glared right back. "Just my cat."

He was taken aback for a second. "Your cat?"

I held my expression. "That's right."

Nobody spoke. Then the older cop handed me his card.

"That's all for now," he said. "If any ideas occur to you, call me. Otherwise, stay where you can be reached. Don't go anywhere outside of home or work without giving me a number where you can be reached."

I was happy to be leaving, but managed a scowl anyway. "You mean I drove all the way down here for this?"

"Well, Thompson," the younger one answered sarcastically. "We could always drive you down to the station, if you're disappointed."

I turned toward the steps.

"No thanks. I was just leaving." I trotted down the stairway to my car. Spike had pulled my San Diego County map from the glove compartment and was systematically tearing it apart with her teeth.

"Dammit, Spike," I sighed.

"There's nothing here," the older man said. "We've looked everywhere."

The man with the mustache fingered his pocket knife. The mattress lay around his feet in shreds.

"He can't stay gone forever."

I felt responsible for Sheila's death. I could have told her I didn't want her to take the case, but I had let her win me over. I wanted to cry, but my eyes just ached instead. Sheila had been so beautiful Friday night. So bubbly and crazy, so proud of herself. I couldn't believe she was gone.

Something else kept eating at me during the drive home. The detective had asked so few questions. I wondered. What evidence could the police have that would point to a second car on the bridge? Could Sheila's death be connected to my Argotech investigation? Probably not, I assured myself. After all, I had told no one of my suspicions, except for Sheila and Penny. No one would have any reason to suspect that I knew anything or that I had gone to see Sheila for that reason. At least no one I could think of . . .

And then another thought occurred to me: the letter. Previt might have figured out somehow that I had the letter. I had left work early on Thursday. Maybe Previt had tried to retrieve the letter, and had put two and two together when he discovered I was missing. I shuddered at the thought that Previt might have followed Sheila from Nolan's.

I told myself to stop thinking so much, but I couldn't help it. I knew I was acting paranoid, but I found myself glancing in the rearview mirror to see who was following me. It was impossible to tell. There were always too many cars heading north on Interstate 5 on a Sunday afternoon—residents of

Los Angeles heading home after a weekend in San Diego. Today was no exception.

As I was carrying Spike up the front steps of my condo, my fears became tangible. The front door was ajar. I was sure I had locked it. I waited several seconds before summoning the courage to peek inside. The place had been ransacked. The sofa, love seat, bookcase, and television were all overturned on the floor. Books were lying helter-skelter among the sofa cushions.

I pushed open the front door and found the other rooms in the same condition. Nothing had been spared. Even my mattress had been slit open and pulled apart, stuffing thrown all over the floor. My clothes were all over the bedroom.

It dawned on me suddenly that I was in danger. Without dropping Spike, I found my suitcase, tossed in only a change of clothing and toiletries, and ran outside to my car.

My fear of being followed was now an obsession. I took detour after detour, winding first west toward the ocean, then north, then back eastward, all the while concentrating on my rearview mirror. I scanned the side streets and driveways, searching for anything even remotely suspicious. I made sudden U-turns, just to see if any other vehicle would appear. The net effect of my efforts was to send Spike careening back and forth across the back seat. There were never any suspicious vehicles. I was always alone.

I could have driven in any direction, but for some reason I headed for Pacific Beach. Maybe my curiosity was as great as my fear. Pacific Beach was the one place central to all the evidence: the Gopher apartment on Crown Point Drive, the Ingraham Street Bridge railing, and Sheila's office on Garnet Avenue.

I drove down to the white wooden roller coaster, less than a hundred yards from the ocean. All around me were the sights and sounds of a city beach: brightly painted food stands catering to surfers and skateboarders; a balloonman and a nearby ice cream truck surrounded by children; an ill-clad wino lying asleep on the grass, his face covered with an open newspaper. People were everywhere. The two lanes of Mission Boulevard were inadequate for all the Sunday traffic.

I parked quickly on the side street nearest the bridge that led to Mission Bay Park. I grabbed my suitcase in one hand and Spike in the other. Hurrying westward, I found the boardwalk along the beach, but there were too many people-watchers along the way. Even among the do-your-own-thing beachgoers of southern California I felt conspicuous carrying a suitcase and a struggling cat. I opted instead for the narrow alleys parelleling the boardwalk. I made certain to avoid any contact with other people.

After two or three miles of wandering through the narrow maze of alleys behind the beach cottages and shops, I reached the Crystal Pier at the western foot of Garnet Avenue. If someone had been following me before, they could not be following me now.

The two men were sipping brandy in the backyard of the mansion, near the pen where the Dobermans were kept. The face of the dark-haired man was stern.

"We should have waited for him to come home. We could have brought him here."

The older man shook his head. "Your Porsche attracts too much attention. He would have noticed it. We took an unacceptable risk going there in the first place."

"So what do you suggest we do now?"

"Find him, bring him here, get the letter."

"And if he won't cooperate?"

"We use the dogs."

The old motel, painted white in classic beachfront fashion, jutted out over the ocean along both sides of the pier, creating a protected boardwalk thirty feet above the ocean breakers. The outlines of a half-dozen fishermen were visible against the horizon at the far end. The motel office was at the entrance, beneath a giant concrete arch with the words "CRYSTAL PIER" painted in sky blue letters against a whitewashed background. I knelt beside the arch, opened my suitcase, and dropped Spike between my underwear and socks. The weight of the lid was enough to keep her from escaping temporarily, although her paw had already found its way through the opening when I laid the suitcase on the planks and walked to the office.

The desk clerk hardly noticed me as I paid for one night and returned to the arch. Spike had already managed to poke her head through the crack in the suitcase. She jumped into my arms as I managed to snap the lid shut. As we approached cottage 19 the sharp smell of freshly caught fish grew stronger, and the surf slapped against the wooden pilings below my feet.

Spike was frightened. Her nails clutched violently at my shirt, and she mewed plaintively with every crash of the waves.

Cottage 19 was a white bungalow with black sailboats painted on the window shutters. Inside, the room was dark and small, and felt almost homemade, like a treehouse. The floor was uneven, emphasizing the queasy movement of the pier as it swayed with the rhythm of the surf. The bed was old, with rusty springs that squeaked horribly when I sat down to place Spike on the floor. A back door led out to a tiny balcony with a view toward the hills of Tijuana in the distance. The bathroom was barely large enough for the toilet and metal shower stall.

I stepped out onto the balcony, enjoying the fresh breeze as it beat against my face. Spike cowered behind my shoes, content to watch my movements from the safety of the motel room. I felt the need to protect her, as though she represented Sheila and all women. I wanted to get a grip on myself—to find some sanity in the events of the last two days.

I remembered the words of one of my professors: *"Start with the facts."*

Fact number one: I had seen a short letter to a company named Gopher. The proposed consulting fee was outrageous, and the letter itself was suspicious for legal and accounting reasons.

Fact number two: The letter had been sent to a residential apartment with no listed telephone number.

Fact number three: Sheila Simmons had been killed in an automobile accident that the police were investigating.

Fact number four: My condo had been ransacked by intruders.

Outside, the ocean roared and the sea gulls cried as I struggled with the pieces of the puzzle. I focused on fact number four. Nothing of value had been taken from my condo. The TV, the VCR, the kitchen appliances—all were thrown about. Why had nothing been taken?

Then it came to me: The mattress had been shredded. I slapped the side of my head. *The letter.* Of course. They had to be looking for the letter. I felt in my jacket for the folded paper. There it was. A single page responsible for so much damage. And then I considered fact number three: If Sheila's death was not an accident, the same murderers would be coming after me.

The detective stood beside a white Chevette. A blonde was in the driver's seat. The younger cop sat beside her. He was no longer in uniform.

"What do we do now?" the woman asked.

The detective's forehead was creased in thought.

"Just watch him for the time being," he said. *"We can move in later tonight."*

It was impossible to take a nap. I kept tossing and turning, unable to quiet the confusion inside my head. Below me the surf was playful and loud, bowling strikes against the wooden pilings. Spike needed a litter box, so I went to find a container to fill with some beach sand. The sun was setting as I stepped outside and turned left toward the bait shop to ask for an empty box. The young clerk was more than happy to oblige. It was one less thing he would have to carry off the pier at the end of the day.

I toted the box toward the motel office and walked down to the beach beneath the pier, scanning the streets and sidewalks in both directions. As I tossed a fistful of sand into the box, I noticed a white car on the street—a Chevy Chevette—with a man and a woman inside. The car caught my eye because it was stopped in the middle of the block with its motor running, and both people were looking at me from behind dark glasses. When I rose up to see them better, they turned away quickly, and the car moved down the street away from the motel.

If I had been in my right mind I would have left the motel right away. But fatigue was clouding my judgment. Despite a brilliant sunset and the cool breeze rushing in from the ocean, I was feeling the burden of the last two days.

Hit men don't drive Chevettes, I reasoned vaguely. The two people were probably tourists.

I finished my digging and trudged back to the cottage.

When I pushed open the cottage door, Spike dive-bombed the litter box from atop the doorframe, spraying sand everywhere.

"Dammit, Spike."

I was too tired to be angry. I was lucky I didn't drop the box. Otherwise, it would have landed on my feet. I set it in the bathroom next to the shower stall and collapsed on the bed without stopping to remove my shoes. I thought of Sheila. As I fell into a deeper sleep my thoughts turned to dreams.

I am seated beside her in the sports car. I can see the terror in her eyes as she wrenches the steering wheel, trying to maintain control. I hear the awful crash of metal against the bridge railing—see her body falling—down, down to the waters of Mission Bay. I listen for her scream, as if the sound of her voice can bring her blue eyes back to life.

But then I was awake. I heard the sounds of the motel. The waves crashing against the pilings below me. The wind whistling past the cottage.

I'm not sure when it happened. I know it was dark outside. The door to the cottage was opening slowly, sending a draft of cold air toward my bed. Then I saw it—the gleam of dark metal. There were no lights on the pier. I could barely see the man's arm easing the door open. I had never faced the barrel of a pistol. I was petrified, unable to cry out.

Chapter IV

The intruder stepped into the room. The silhouette of a man's head was all I could see. In that instant, a furry blur plunged from atop the doorframe.

Spike! I thought. Not now!

An explosion from the pistol shook the room. The intruder jerked his arm backward and ran out the door. I jumped out of bed in time to see a shadowy figure racing to the end of the pier and down the street.

I switched on the light and looked around. Spike was huddled near the litter box, shivering with fright. There was a single bullet hole in the ceiling above the bed. I glanced at my watch. Three-thirty. I splashed some cold water on my face, grabbed Spike and the suitcase, and headed outside.

The air seemed especially cold. The intruder could have been nearby but I had no choice. There was only one exit from the pier, and that was toward the street. I was not about to attempt a thirty-foot drop into the Pacific Ocean with a suitcase and a cat. I stayed close to the cottages on the right side, but I was unsure whether to move slowly, giving myself a chance to scan the street, or run as fast as I could to present a more difficult target. I managed both. I scanned slowly for a few careful steps, then broke into a run.

Spike wasn't helping. Her sharp claws tore into my chest and neck, but I was too scared to think about the pain. My eyes were focused on the end of the pier, and my mind was already deciding which way to run. Apparently, no one had heard the shot. The cottages and the motel office were silent and dark as I flew past.

When I reached land I cut sharply to my left and dashed along the sand. The private property fronting the beach was bounded by fences and hedges, so a pursuer would have to stay close to the water to follow me. Since there was no one behind me I knew I was not being followed. At least not yet.

I kept glancing backward. I must have run at least three miles. Finally, out of sheer exhaustion, I stopped, panting heavily as I dropped Spike and the suitcase onto a clump of seaweed. The crash of ocean breakers drowned out all the other night sounds, and the only light came from the infrequent streetlamps near the buildings on the cliffs. My eyes had adjusted to the dim light, but they were burning from the cold, salty wind that had beat against my face as I ran. I saw no signs of life. Nothing was moving except Spike and the water.

A few hundred feet inland, I could just make out the shadows of a cliff. I decided Spike and I could spend the rest of the night there in relative safety. I used a large rock and my suitcase to block the breeze as best I could. Spike huddled closer to me than she had ever wanted to before. The fatigue in my muscles and bones and the steady roar of the ocean lulled me back to a fitful sleep.

The detective in the green sedan pulled up next to the white Chevette.

"Well? How did it go?"

The blonde in the driver's seat shouted back. "We lost him! Can you believe it?"

The young cop beside her looked sheepish. "He had someone in the room with him. Hit my arm. Made the gun go off. I didn't figure on two people."

The detective scratched his head. "Which way did they go?"

"Only one of them came out of the room," said the blonde. "He ran down to the beach. I lost sight of him after that."

"He probably went north," the detective said. "He'd want to stay away from the streetlights. I'll go up to Bird Rock, where the cliffs end. You two stay here in case the other guy comes out."

"And what if he doesn't?" the younger man asked.

"Give him ten minutes," answered the detective. "Then move in. When you finish up here I'll need you up the coast."

It was past eight o'clock by the time the gray sun found its way through the shadows to my groggy face. I saw a jogger pass below me near the breakers. The tide had receded since last night.

Spike was no longer beside me—she was stalking a sea gull fifty yards away. I left her alone. I had my own problems, with wet sand caked all over my legs. I felt dirty, wrinkled, and unshaven. I pulled a clean shirt and blue jeans from my suitcase and dressed quickly behind the rock where we had slept. Then I went after Spike. She was not easy to catch, but she finally surrendered when I pretended to have some food in my hand. Once again, we started up the beach.

After about fifteen minutes of steady walking, I found a set of concrete rest rooms, and carried Spike in with me. I handed her one of my wet socks to play with while I tried my hand at shaving without a mirror. I didn't have much luck, since my mind was wandering. I was trying to decide where to go next.

I was leery of contacting the police. They might still consider me a suspect. The last thing I needed was to be jailed by the detective for disobeying his order to stay home. Even if I tried to explain my suspicions about Previt, I had too few provable facts to make anything stick. The letter would mean nothing to the police. The fact that a burglar had shot at me would only prove that I was somebody's target. At best I might convince the police to provide me with some protection for a few days. But then what? I had no job, no friends, and no place to sleep.

And then it hit me: Augustus Martin. Why hadn't I thought of him before?

I remembered back to when I first met Augustus Martin in high school. Even then he was too fat and too tall to blend into the background the way he wanted to. We had attended high school together in Ocracoke. He was the only black kid in the entire school system, but he tried hard not to be noticed. My guess is that he was driven underground in junior high by unmerciful taunting aimed at his fat, black body.

"Fat" might be the wrong word, for he was certainly no heavier than his six-foot-six-inch frame would warrant. "Soft" and "slow" might be more accurate. In gym class the boys would laugh at the way his skin jiggled when he ran. But he always dressed neatly—especially neatly for the late sixties.

It was "Augustus"; always "Augustus." Never "Gus" or "Augie." As if the stork's random demographics were not cruel enough—burying him within layers of minority classifications in a southern town—he was orphaned before the age of three and was raised in England by a white woman named Hazel Whittington, who brought Augustus to America after the death of her husband. They lived in a beach cottage near the Ocracoke lighthouse. It was Hazel who insisted that he be addressed by his formal given name.

Augustus and I were seated next to each other in twelfth-grade physics lab. Even though there were only twelve of us in the class, we were paired off in two-seater desks facing the teacher. It was in that laboratory that I first began to admire the piece of work God had wrought in Augustus Martin's brain.

It was not so much that his mind was uncluttered or his work habits organized. To the contrary, everything about him seemed mysterious and confused. During the lecture on gravity, for example, I remember glancing over at Augustus's notebook. He had divided the page into five sections. Each was labeled with a word drawn from the teacher's lecture. For example, one section was labeled "gravity," one was "acceleration," and one was "mass." Inside the sections were pictures resembling hieroglyphics. At the bottom of the page was a single phrase: "need 2 RF3 capacitors, 30 ft cu wire."

As the lecture progressed, the page grew more ornate, with diagrams and arrows linking the pictures, and more lines dividing the sections into subsections. By the end of the lecture, I found that I had taken nearly ten pages of notes. Augustus, on the other hand, had finished the lecture with one page resembling a line drawing of seaweed.

At that time in my life I was too self-conscious of Augustus's social stigmas to ask him any questions. Like most adolescent males I was dominated by fear of rejection. If word had gotten around that I was friendly with Augustus Martin, God only knows what horrible things could have happened. I might have been turned down the next time I called a special girl for a date. She might have said, "I hear you hang out with Augustus Martin," and I would have had no choice but to jump off the lighthouse.

The spring term of our senior year was different, though. The sixties were changing life in the South. Forbidden things became curious and exciting. A what-the-hell attitude was replacing our fears.

It was in the spring of 1970 when I finally asked Augustus about his notes. Even a question that innocuous was difficult for me, facing, as I did, his awesome stigma and substantial physical attributes. His chubby lower lip rested in a state of permanent pout, a condition that served only to put off further those few people who would have approached him. Perhaps as a hint of the complexity that lay within him, and as a counterpoint to all else about my large black friend, his brown eyes sparkled, and I could only guess that he had discovered some secret of life hidden from the rest of us—some secret that enabled him to cut through all the prejudice, hate, and cultural stereotyping, and focus squarely on the pure, intellectual delight of physics and math. I swallowed deeply and gave it a try.

"Uh, Gus . . .," I began.

"Augustus," he grunted.

"Uh, yeah, okay, Augustus. I was wondering about your notes, what all the lines and pictures are about."

Augustus sat silently for a few seconds, unsure, I think, whether or not to share secrets with one too slow to figure things out for himself.

"They are diagrams of the lecture, of course." He spoke in a formal version of the King's English he had inherited from Hazel, except that years of growing up in Ocracoke had corrupted his dialect with strains of a Carolina tidal drawl. It became obvious after a few embarrassing seconds that he had finished talking, but I refused to give up that easily.

"I know that much, Augustus, but it seems I take five or ten pages of notes, while you get by with one page of pictures and arrows."

He sighed with such emotional fervor that I thought the heavens might open.

"Well," he continued reluctantly, "it would not be hard to understand my methodology if you were to peruse the correct chapter before each class."

He pulled what looked like a large book from his knapsack.

"My mother purchased this treatise at a used bookstore in London for two shillings," he said. "It is quite superior to the textbook we were issued in class. Having read the proper chapter, I can surmise what the professor is likely to say. Therefore, I need only draw a few illustrations to prevent myself from falling asleep."

My mouth must have dropped open, because Augustus laughed before he continued.

"If you follow the tracings on each of my note pages you can determine the order of the lecture and the number of times the professor referred to each of the subjects represented by my illustrations. Before the examination, I simply count up the arrows leading to each of my illustrations and I know which subjects the professor emphasized in class."

I felt like I was talking to an encyclopedia.

"Don't you have a hard time finding all the formulas in a thick book? Or do you memorize the book, while you read it?" My questions were quite serious. Augustus's speech and methods were so otherworldly to me, I would have believed him if he told me he memorized the textbook in one sitting. Instead, he laughed again.

"Actually my memory is rather inadequate. The formulas are not difficult because I use them in my work."

"What kind of work?"

Augustus grinned like a mule eating briars. It was the first time I had ever seen his teeth.

"You should be most welcome to come to my home after school if you wish. I doubt I could explain everything to your satisfaction now."

The teacher entered the room. Augustus reached into his knapsack, pulling out his black notebook filled with pictures and arrows—a notebook that now seemed childishly simple, yet wonderfully profound.

That was the beginning. I visited the home of Augustus Martin and his "mother," Hazel Whittington, at least a dozen times in the spring of 1970.

There, I learned of his great interest in everything chemical, mechanical, and electronic. The basement of the house was strewn with gadgets and gizmos: old disassembled radios, an open television set, two or three lawn mower engines, and a stack of pipe cut to various lengths. When I asked about the pipes, he informed me that he was perfecting a telescopic listening device.

"It is similar to the 'big ear' used by television networks in games of American football," he said. "The sound technician focuses on the quarterback shouting the signals to his teammates. Listeners at home hear everything as if they were standing on the field."

"I've seen those things on the sidelines," I said. "But they look like giant loudspeakers. Why do you need all the pipes?"

"The big-ear systems are forms of parabolic focusing," he explained. "They are quaint in theory but difficult to construct. It is the parabola which poses the problem. I attempted utilizing various automobile headlight sockets I found at a refuse disposal, however they were too small to accomplish much sound amplification. Instead, I cut these pipes to different lengths at exact specifications, like organ pipes, arranged them in a bundle so that they all aim in exactly the same direction, and attached a microphone at the end."

I was trying to follow his meaning but my eyes must have glazed over. Augustus saw the look on my face and tried again, using simpler language.

"My system works on the same principle as holding a cardboard tube up to one eye while you close the other eye. Everything is shut out except the target you see through the tube. If I insulate the inside and outside of the pipes, the only sounds passing through to the microphone will be the ones generated by my target. All I need now is an amplifier and a set of filters, or a frequency equalizer, to remove extraneous noise."

I was beginning to catch on.

"You mean you could filter out dogs barking and music playing and just listen to two people talking?"

"Exactly."

A few weeks after our graduation from high school, Hazel and Augustus moved to San Diego to be closer to Hazel's sister. Augustus was accepted at Cal Tech, which meant nothing to us in Ocracoke at the time. Although I knew he lived nearby when I moved to Solana Beach, I had never looked him up during my two years in California. Little did I know that the sound equipment developed by Augustus Martin in high school would one day spell the difference between my survival and death.

I found a pay phone a few yards from the bathhouse. Augustus was indeed home, happy to hear from me, and happy to take a day off from work to listen to my problems. His voice hadn't changed in fifteen years. I was hoping his brain hadn't changed either.

With a second quarter I called a taxi, giving the dispatcher an address near the pay phone. I carried Spike to the top of the hill overlooking the beach. To my right, I saw the white Chevette moving slowly along the street fronting the water. The cab arrived a few minutes later, and Spike and I were speeding out of Pacific Beach.

The driver stopped at a white stucco home on a tree-lined street in North Park. This was working-class San Diego, a neighborhood where people washed their cars on Sundays and spent evenings with the lights on and curtains raised, TVs blaring and children banging screen doors as they ran to play with the neighbors' children out in the alley. I paid the cabdriver and carried Spike and my suitcase up the walkway to the front porch.

Hazel Whittington answered the door with her two cats. Her white hair was tied in a bun.

"Why, Michael Thompson! It's good to see you! And you brought a cat! How wonderful! What's its name?"

"Spike," I answered, as I gave Hazel a big hug. "I hope you don't mind me bringing her in. Do you think they'll be jealous?" I pointed to her two cats.

"Of course not." She lifted the furry monster from my arms. "Come on, Spike, let's go down to the basement and show Augustus who's here."

After Hazel had retreated upstairs to fix some coffee, Augustus and I caught up on the last fifteen years. He had obtained his Ph.D. in physics from Cal Tech and landed a high-paying job with General Dynamics. After a few years of "the bloody rat race" he found a less stressful position in a small defense firm similar to Argotech.

He was now, as he put it, "happy as a big black clam," and flashed me one of his wide, contagious grins. Fifteen years had done nothing to change his appearance. If anything, he seemed happier and younger, as if the years in southern California had worked a preservative miracle on his skin.

Hazel returned with two mugs of steaming coffee and excused herself again. Augustus soon changed the subject.

"And what is it about you being in trouble?"

I explained to him as much as I could, beginning with the letter, which I showed him, and ending with the attempt on my life at the motel. He was especially interested in the two people I had seen in the white Chevette.

"Any idea who they were?" he asked.

I shook my head.

"Not a clue. Before the burglar hit last night I figured they were a couple of tourists. I couldn't imagine Previt hiring somebody to follow me in a Chevette."

Augustus nodded in agreement as I sipped some coffee and continued.

"Maybe they *were* tourists, for all I know. Anyway, whoever tracked me down at the hotel must have E.S.P. There's no way I could have been followed. I was watching every second in all directions."

"Except under the automobile," muttered Augustus under his breath.

"Except where?" I asked.

"Under the auto," he repeated in his British-Carolina drawl. "Anybody could have placed a remote transmitter near the axle to monitor your movements. They could have followed you from a mile away and you'd not have known it. Once they determined where you parked, the rest would have been child's play."

"Not so fast," I said. "I stayed clear of people after I left the car. No one saw which way I went."

Augustus waved his finger in front of me.

"It was child's play, I must repeat. There are fewer than six motels within walking distance of your parking place. Your pursuers had only to question a few employees. You are not hard for a clerk to remember; you are almost as tall as I am, and you were carrying a suitcase and a cat."

I slapped my forehead with the palm of my hand. "I can't believe I was so stupid."

The room was quiet while we both thought about the situation. Augustus broke the silence.

"Our first step should be to visit the motel office. Whoever followed you there probably asked about you. Maybe we can get a description of your pursuers from the clerk."

I finished my last gulp of coffee.

"Augustus," I said. "Are you sure you want to get involved in all this?"

He looked away awkwardly. I had never seen such a troubled look on his face.

"When we were in high school," he began slowly, "you were the only friend I had. We have been out of high school for fifteen years and I haven't had any real friends since then."

The pout I remembered from long ago returned to his face. I stared at him in wonder, but I was feeling guilty. In high school Augustus was only a curiosity to me. I had never considered him an important friend, or even a real person. When it was time for me to head off to college, I never gave our friendship a second thought. I simply forgot he existed and focused on my own future.

He changed the subject as if I had never asked the question.

"Our second step should be to visit Mr. Terrell on Crown Point Drive," he said. "Ms. Simmons would have begun her investigation there, although she probably should have known that was unnecessary."

"Why do you say that?" I asked.

"Because it is clear the letter was written solely to create a paper trail for Argotech's auditors. There is doubtless no such person as James Terrell."

I shrugged my shoulders.

"The third place we need to visit," he continued, "is the bridge where Ms. Simmons was killed. I should like to examine the skid marks before they are obscured by traffic."

"Sounds like we have a full day ahead—"

"I have not finished," Augustus interrupted. "We must find out the time and place of Ms. Simmons's funeral. We must arrive in such a way that no one sees us."

I just stared back at him, wondering what ideas were already at work in his magnificent brain.

Chapter V

Hazel met us at the top of the stairway. She was stroking Spike behind the ears.

"You didn't tell me Spike was a climber!" She giggled. "I put her on the floor to play with Tigger and Jinx and she shot right up the drapes to the top of the door. It was all I could do to get her down."

"I forgot to warn you about that," I said, laughing. "She's also got a bad habit of jumping on your head when you open the door."

"Come on, Michael, we'd best get moving," Augustus interrupted. It dawned on me that he was afraid I'd start talking about Spike and the motel burglar, and that might worry Hazel. He opened the door and motioned me outside.

"We might be late for dinner tonight, Mum."

I had forgotten that Augustus referred to her

that way. I never got used to it, even in the old days when I was spending more time around his house.

"You boys stay out of trouble," she replied. "Michael, don't you worry about Spike. I'll take good care of her."

Augustus led me to a Studebaker that must have been at least thirty years old. The smell of the interior reminded me of the smell of the old 1936 Plymouth my grandmother used to drive. I couldn't help poking fun at the old car.

"You won't be driving too fast, will you?" I teased. "I'm not sure my heart can stand the excitement." I pretended to brace myself against the dashboard as Augustus adjusted the manual transmission on the steering column.

"You had better enjoy this ride while you can," he snorted. "We shall be leaving this automobile at the market."

He drove to a Safeway a few blocks away and pulled into an open space.

"What's the idea?" I asked.

Augustus gave me one of his mule-faced grins. "Oh, ye of little faith."

Augustus led me past the store entrance to the pay phone. I listened as he called a cab and gave the dispatcher our location. Then he looked at me with a maddening, impish expression.

"We can use your car. It would be a pity to let it rust all day at the ocean." He was taking great pleasure in my puzzlement.

"So why didn't we call a cab from your house?"

"The reasons should be obvious," he said. "I had no intention of concerning Mum, and I did not wish the cabdriver to know my address."

"But what about the transmitter on my car?"

"My dear Michael," he said, shaking his head disapprovingly. "If a transmitter can be installed, it can be removed."

A yellow taxi crept across the parking lot toward the main entrance.

"You get in first," Augustus suggested. "Sometimes they drive away if they see a black man approaching."

When we were heading for Mission Bay I turned toward Augustus and asked quietly, "You mind telling me now why we have to do things this way?"

Augustus sighed for effect. "Since you insist."

He turned his head to look out the window a few seconds, stalling between phrases to extract the maximum mileage from my anxiety.

"I want to confirm my suspicion about the transmitter. I also want to see what kind of device it is, so that I can understand the people with whom we shall be dealing. It might also help me to know what kind of equipment our friends are using. If they are using certain kinds of older equipment, it should be easy to pick out their car on the street. I shall be able to identify the antenna. If they are using more sophisticated components, I shall be more worried, but I shall also know more about their tactical philosophy."

I had no idea what he was talking about, but I nodded anyway.

When we were within a few blocks of my car, Augustus spoke to the driver.

"You may stop here. We shall walk the rest of the way."

The driver pulled over by a fire hydrant. Augustus wasted no time jumping out of the cab and running down a small alley behind a liquor store. I paid the driver and followed him.

After a few yards or so we reached an intersection with another alley. Around us was a maze of narrow passageways serving as tiny residential streets. This was the town of Mission Beach—a densely populated community of transient youth, unemployed beach bums, and elderly locals—lying on the narrow strip of land between the Pacific Ocean and Mission Bay.

Most of the houses were no larger than one room each, but they were personalized. Nearby, a cottage painted bright pink with violet trim adjoined a similar hut with dilapidated walls and peeling paint. There were incongruities at every turn.

Augustus stopped near the white picket fence surrounding a cottage slightly larger than a child's playhouse.

"I think we have gone far enough," he said. "We can traverse the alley over there, which should parallel the street where your auto is parked. The closer we come to it, the more we must be alert to strangers. Try to watch one person at a time to determine who might be watching your auto. Remain at least one-half block behind me. Now describe your auto."

I put one hand on the fence. "It's a blue Buick Riviera. Brand-new. Still has the dealer's plates."

Augustus held out his hand. "Where are your keys?"

I fished them out of my pocket.

"When you see me start the engine," he said, "observe all the people on the street. Notice whether anyone is watching me. I shall pick you up on Mission Boulevard two blocks north of the roller coaster, but you must permit me about ten minutes. I shall attempt to lose anyone who might be following."

I handed Augustus the keys and watched as he lumbered down the alley toward the street. When he disappeared around the corner, I trailed him from a distance. A few minutes later I saw my car on the far side of the street, still parked where I had left it.

Remembering Augustus's instructions, I began observing the people within eyesight of my car. There were not many: a young man and woman wheeling a baby stroller toward the beach; a group of teenaged surfers exiting a Volkswagen bug; and an elderly bag lady pushing a shopping cart full of plastic sacks. No one else was in sight.

Augustus walked casually down the sidewalk on the opposite side of the street, passed by my car without looking at it, and performed a clumsy about-face. After two huge strides he knelt beside my car, then rose, looked around, and trotted toward the Volkswagen. Then he walked back to my car, got in on the driver's side, and gunned the car away from the curb.

I looked around to see who was watching. The street was deserted now except for the bag lady, who seemed oblivious to the world beyond her shopping cart. I ran back to the alley in the direction of Mission Boulevard, killing ten minutes by wandering up one passageway and down another, trying not to attract attention to myself. Then I headed for the street. No sooner had I stepped out onto Mission Boulevard than Augustus pulled over to the curb.

"Get in quick," he shouted.

I opened the door and jumped in. Augustus drove about two miles before either of us said a word.

"Tell me what you saw back there," he said.

"Nothing," I answered.

"Good." Augustus smiled. "I saw nothing myself. I can assure you this time that we will not be followed. The transmitter was just as I had hoped—an old General Systems model. It can transmit up to five miles, but it is only two hundred yards accurate at that distance. In other words, your pursuers knew your general direction and distance, but not your exact location."

Augustus pulled the car into the parking lot of a Denny's Restaurant and switched off the engine.

"So why is that important to us now?" I asked.

Augustus sighed. "What it means is that our friends will have no idea the transmitter is no longer on your car. Since I only moved it a few yards, their receiver will not detect any movement even if they are paying close attention, which I doubt."

Augustus was giving me only the barest of explanations. We were now within shouting distance of the Crystal Pier, however, and I was in no mood for games.

"Look, Augustus," I said with a trace of irritation. "I appreciate all the help you're giving me, but don't you understand we could both be killed? We really didn't need to get my car just so you could play with the transmitter."

A wise, sad expression returned to his face.

"My dear Michael," he said. "I realize you have been subjected to a great amount of stress, but you really mustn't jump to conclusions. You failed to appreciate the simple fact that I was able to move the transmitter to the Volkswagen. Your friends should be rather surprised when they discover they are trailing three La Jolla surfers."

Augustus led the way to the Crystal Pier Motel office. Inside, I recognized the elderly clerk who had checked me in the day before.

"Won't have no vacancy 'til after three," he said politely. "Not sure even then if we'll have one."

"We're not checking in," I said. "I'm checking out. Room nineteen. I locked myself out this morning. I need a spare key to see if I left anything."

The old man searched through a pile of cards on the counter.

"What's the name?" he asked.

"Barron," I said, giving him the false name I had used the day before.

"Here you go." He handed me a room key. "Better hurry, though, checkout is in fifteen minutes."

Charles Previt leaned across the desk of his boss, Robert Goren. The clatter of computer printers outside the office masked their conversation, but Previt spoke quietly nonetheless.

"No one's seen him since he left work Thursday afternoon."

He fingered his mustache nervously. Goren rose from his swivel chair and walked slowly to the cabinet in the corner. He opened the sliding door, revealing a marble counter and several decanters.

"Bourbon or Scotch?" he asked without turning around.

Previt didn't answer.

Goren found an empty glass and poured a finger of bourbon. He motioned for Previt to take it.

"I don't need it," Previt said, his firm jaw motionless.

"Just take it," Goren said.

Previt stepped toward Goren and grabbed the bourbon. Goren returned to his desk and opened the top drawer. He pulled out an automatic pistol and handed it to Previt.

"One of my boys found it in Mexico," he said. "No registration, no previous owners."

Previt set the glass down and rolled the gun around in his hands. "I thought we decided to buy him off."

Goren shook his head. "Not unless we have to. This way's cleaner if we do it right."

Previt ran his thumb along the smooth barrel, his dark eyes filled with silent hate.

"So where do we find him?" he asked.

Goren smiled. "I got the funeral arrangements on the Simmons girl."

Previt looked puzzled. "What's that got to do with Thompson?"

Goren returned to his desk and sat down. "Word has it that he might have been hot for the girl. I'd say the odds are decent he'll show up at the funeral."

Previt nodded. "And if he does, I kill the son of a bitch."

The motel room was just as I had left it. Augustus climbed on the bed and stuck his forefinger in the bullet hole.

"See if you can locate a knife," he said.

I found a steak knife in the kitchenette and handed it up to him. I watched him widen the bullet hole by scraping around it with the knife. A few seconds later the bullet dropped into his outstretched palm.

"It's a large caliber," he said. "Thirty-eight or forty-five. Your friend was not joking." He climbed down from the bed. "We must speak to the old man again—ask him if anyone came looking for you yesterday."

In a few minutes we were back at the motel office. The clerk had moved from behind the counter and was standing in the front doorway. Augustus remained well behind me as we approached.

"Here's your keys," I called to him. "Say, do you remember anyone asking for me yesterday?"

The man took the keys and walked back inside the office.

"Well, let's see," he began slowly. "My memory's not too good these days. But there was one lady. Kind of fat with a head full of blond hair and big sunglasses. You know, the kind with the mirrors. There was a big guy with her. Must have been twice her size. He had on glasses too, except his were dark."

I noted the descriptions carefully.

"And you say they were asking for me?"

The man shook his head. "Not exactly. The only reason I remember them is they didn't know quite who they were looking for. Said they were friends of a man who had just checked in. Described you pretty well, but said your name was Johnson or Thompson or something. When I told them that a Mr. Barron was the only single who had checked in, the girl asked me which room. I told her room nineteen and the girl says, 'Sorry, I guess we got the wrong place.' Didn't make no sense."

"About how tall was the girl?" I asked.

The man held out his hand just below his nose, indicating a height of about five feet two inches.

"Thank you," Augustus said as we turned to leave. "You have a very nice motel."

Our next stop was the apartment building on Crown Point Drive. We parked near the front entrance and walked up the steps. The mailman was in the lobby, sorting letters into panels of pigeonholes. He was the same man I had seen when I had pretended to be James Terrell. A flash of inspiration struck me, so I motioned for Augustus to keep quiet.

"Hi! My name's James Terrell," I said. "I spoke to you last Friday. I was wondering if you remember talking to a sexy redhead around here last Saturday."

The mailman stopped what he was doing and turned around to face me.

"Redhead? You bet I remember. She caused all kinds of trouble. Who was she, anyway?"

"She's my wife?" I lied. "I'd really appreciate it if you could tell me what happened. I hope she didn't run into my brother."

"Your brother?" He scratched his head. "So that explains it."

Augustus and I looked at each other, then back at the mailman, who continued. "She comes up to me, just like you did, except I was finishing up the last of the mail for this building. She says she's Mrs. James Terrell and she's supposed to pick up the mail for Mr. Terrell. Sure enough, there was one letter for you at the bottom of the stack. She takes the letter and walks outside to this little red sports car."

He pointed to the street.

"Well, that's when it all started. This man in a three-piece suit walks right in and says his name is Terrell and asks if I have any mail for him. By this time I figure I'm going crazy, what with everybody named Terrell all asking for the same thing. Anyway, I tell him I just handed the letter to his wife, and I pointed to the lady in the red sports car. He says, 'What wife? I don't have a wife,' and heads down the steps toward the lady. Well, then she looks up and sees this guy coming, so she peels right out of there. Then he jumps in his car."

"What kind of car?" I asked.

"I don't know. One of those fancy German types. It was black. Anyway, that's the last I saw of them. I should have figured he was your brother. That explains why he had the same name. Didn't look much like you, though."

"What did he look like?" I asked.

"Black hair, mustache," the man said, rubbing his forehead.

"That's my brother all right," I said.

"Your family always act that way?" the mailman asked.

Augustus broke in. "The Terrells have always been rather strange. Especially at that time of the month when the family inheritance check arrives."

I stifled a snort and spun toward the door. Augustus followed me outside.

"That was Previt," I said to Augustus as he started the car.

"Who, the mailman?" he asked.

"No. The man with the black mustache. Previt drives a black Porsche and wears three-piece suits."

Augustus drove slowly away from the apartments.

"That's good news and bad news," he said. "The good news is that Previt was operating alone. That means we are not dealing with a large organization like the Mafia. Otherwise, Previt would have sent an errand boy to retrieve the letter."

I nodded. "What's the bad news?"

"My dear Michael," he continued. "It appears as though you have stumbled upon Mr. Previt's little scheme to embezzle three million dollars from his own company. People kill people for less money than that."

"I think he gave me that message the other night," I agreed, thinking back to the motel room.

"There is just one thing I cannot understand," Augustus said as we turned left onto Pacific Beach Drive.

"What's that?"

"The letters," he responded. "Why would he write two letters? One letter seems unlikely enough in an embezzlement scheme. But a second letter seems incredibly stupid, especially when the author arranges to retrieve it himself."

I found the question just as baffling as Augustus did. When we had traveled a few blocks, he slowed the car to a crawl.

"I shall follow the route to the bridge that Sheila most likely followed. She was trying to elude Previt and she enjoyed a small head start, but her Fiat would have been no match for his Porsche. We might be able to find some tire marks where Sheila made her turns."

As Augustus predicted, there were skid marks at several corners. Augustus stopped the car at each place and I was obliged to jump out of the car with him to examine the marks more closely.

"This one belonged to the Fiat," he said, pointing to a set of blurred tracks. "And this was the Porsche."

The difference was slight, but the tread designs were distinctive.

"How do you know these marks weren't made by two other cars?" I asked.

"Too much of a coincidence," he replied. "What are the odds that a random pair of cars left the apartment building recently and left tire tracks at all the same corners? Given the mail carrier's testimony, we can safely infer that these marks were made by the Fiat and Porsche."

We got back in the car and followed the twisting route to the bridge. My mind raced with thoughts of Sheila. I pictured her brown freckles and the way she hugged me with excitement when I told her she was hired. I remembered my dream about her accident, believing I was in the car with her as she raced along the bridge.

. . . she wrenches the steering wheel to the left, trying to maintain control, but instead I hear the awful crash of metal against the bridge railing . . .

"Look out!" I screamed.

"What is it?" Augustus stiffened his grip on the steering wheel. "What's the matter?"

"Nothing," I said, shuddering. "Sorry, I must have been daydreaming."

Chapter VI

Augustus drove past the damaged railing to the other side of the bridge and found an empty space in a parking lot close to the water. After my outburst his manner had changed. His lip was set in its familiar pout, but now his eyes were intense.

Neither of us spoke as we left the car and walked toward the bridge. The closer we came to the accident site the more I felt overwhelmed by the pressure of Sheila's murder.

We found a narrow construction corridor just inside the railing. Ignoring signs warning "NO PEDESTRIAN TRAFFIC," we headed up the ramp. The northbound traffic whizzed by us at fifty miles per hour, separated from us by only a few inches of temporary railing—the same plywood that had failed to stop Sheila's Fiat. Augustus stopped when we reached a spot a hundred yards from the summit of the bridge. A pair of parallel skid marks began near the top of the bridge and veered directly toward us.

"We must go farther up," Augustus said, motioning toward the marks.

"What are you talking about?" I shouted above the roar of the traffic. "We'll be killed if we step out there."

"I said nothing about stepping out there," Augustus chided, "I said we must go farther up. I want to see what happens to those tracks where they begin."

I shrugged my shoulders in defeat, following Augustus in the tight space along the rail until we could clearly see the start of the skid marks. We were standing at the highest point of the bridge.

"There!" Augustus gestured toward a flurry of marks that began at the foot of the bridge and swerved into the northbound lanes at three distinct places. "That's why your police detective called this a murder. I fail to see how anyone could disagree."

A city bus strained past us, temporarily interrupting our view.

"Notice the extra set of tracks," Augustus continued. "That's where the Porsche was forcing the Fiat into the northbound lane. He could not have pushed too hard without risking an accident himself. He was probably hoping the Fiat would crash into an oncoming vehicle."

"So what made her go off the bridge?" I asked.

Augustus pointed to the starting point of the final swerve marks.

"The Porsche made one last, heavy push against the Fiat right here at the top. For the smaller car, the change from moving uphill to downhill rendered the steering much more difficult. The tendency of a body in motion is to follow a straight line."

I vaguely remembered that law from our physics class.

"The direction of the Fiat would therefore have been straight off the bridge," Augustus said. "Her steering wheel would be worthless in the midst of a skid."

We walked to the broken section of the bridge, where the Fiat fell over the edge.

"The marks from the rear tires end here," Augustus said, "well short of the railing."

"Which means . . . ?" I began.

"Which means she very nearly stopped," Augustus answered. "Had she been traveling faster, the marks would continue to the edge. Instead, they stop just short, suggesting that the automobile was no longer skidding when the front tires went over."

"You mean she stopped the car right on the edge?"

"The evidence will support no other theory. She had a few seconds in which to watch the Fiat tip over the rail."

"How horrible!"

"Quite."

Augustus studied the red paint on the railing that had scraped from Sheila's car.

"Unfortunately, this entire bridge is under construction," he said. "The railing she hit would not hold a motorcycle."

I bit my lip, imagining Sheila's horror as she fell into the water below her. There was nothing more for us to see, so Augustus and I began our descent from the bridge. About halfway down the ramp, Augustus slowed his pace.

"Michael," he said in a low voice, as though the passing cars could hear us, "do not be conspicuous, but take a look at your car."

After a few steps I glanced quickly in the direction of the parking lot. A chubby blonde was climbing into the driver's side of a white Chevette parked directly adjacent to my Buick. A muscular, dark-haired man jumped in beside her. The car moved quickly out of the parking lot, turning south away from the bridge.

"Well . . . ?" Augustus asked, after the Chevette had disappeared in the distance.

"That's the car I saw at the Crystal Pier," I answered.

By the time we reached the parking lot Augustus was marching ten strides ahead of me, his scientific curiosity strained to the breaking point. When I caught up to him he was bending down beside my car.

"How boring," he laughed, holding a small metal contraption for my inspection. "It is the same brand as the last one they used. They must have a supply of them."

I studied the strange-looking device.

"Why would they plant another transmitter if they know we found the first one?" I asked.

Augustus twirled the device around in his fingers.

"They may assume the other one fell off without our knowledge," he answered. "Are you in the mood for a bit of levity?"

He looked up at me.

"A bit of what?" I asked.

"Fun," he said.

I shrugged my shoulders. "Why not? We're only investigating a murder." I was feeling only half-sarcastic.

"I believe this is one trick you will enjoy," he said, ignoring my comment. His eyes sparkled. "Do you happen to carry any waterproof containers?"

I opened the trunk of my car and pulled out a box of clear plastic Baggies I used to wrap around my camera on rainy days.

He examined the package. "These will work perfectly."

He placed the transmitter in one of the Baggies and walked down to the water. A small motorboat was retrieving a fallen water-skier near the shore. Augustus called out to the boat driver and motioned for him to come closer. The driver obliged, maneuvering the craft in a wide circle that brought the boat and the skier to within a few yards of us.

"Excuse me!" Augustus called, addressing the skier. "We are scientists from Scripps Institute. We are performing a research project involving sonar detection."

He held up the transmitter, which was still visible inside the Baggie.

"Would you mind attaching this transmitter to your life jacket for a short while?"

"No problem!" the skier replied. "Always happy to have an audience."

"That would be marvelous," Augustus replied. He leaned out over the water to hand the beeper to the skier, who stuffed it inside his vest.

"Oh yes, I almost forgot," Augustus continued. "Are you able to hold the tow rope with one hand?"

The skier winked at the boat driver, who answered the question for him.

"Jim here was the runner-up in last year's California Open Waterskiing Championship," the driver said. "This year we expect him to win. If you want him to ski barefoot he can do that too."

Augustus laughed. "That will not be necessary. My friend and I will be driving around the bay to test the range of our receiver. Another pair of scientists will be taking our place in a few minutes. When you see a white Chevette pull up here, be sure to wave to the new scientists so that they can confirm our readings. Then drop the transmitter in the water."

The skier scratched his head.

"Wait a minute, mister. Let me get this straight. You want me to drop this piece of equipment in the middle of Mission Bay? How much does this thing cost?"

"You needn't worry about a thing!" Augustus called back over the revving of the boat motor. "We scientists carry dozens of transmitters. They are equipped with electronic thermometers so we can monitor the water temperature at the bottom of the bay."

The skier shrugged his shoulders. I turned my head and snickered.

"Makes sense, I guess," the skier said. "Glad to help."

He waved at us as the boat driver moved slowly forward, tightening the slack of the tow line.

Augustus opened the driver's door of the Buick and I handed him the keys.

"Let us see how this plays out," he chuckled, apparently unable to contain his enthusiasm.

"I'm getting a reading!" the man shouted.

The blonde swung the Chevette over to the curb. They watched the red light as the compass dial swung sharply to the east.

"They're heading back toward Crown Point!" cried the blonde. "This time we won't lose them."

The tires squealed as she spun the car around in a frantic U-turn.

"Now they're heading back west again," the man said. "They must be driving like maniacs."

"Don't worry," said the blonde. "It's just a Buick. I can keep up with them."

"Hold on a second," the man said. "Now they're moving north."

We drove across the bridge, past the scene of Sheila's murder. We followed the bay all the way around to the west until we reached the alley neighborhoods of Mission Beach. At that point Augustus parked and walked around to the rear of the car.

"I saw one pair of binoculars and one camera with a telephoto lens in here," he said, opening the trunk as I got out to join him. "I shall take the binoculars while you hold the camera. You may wish to photograph the water-skier at the appropriate time. You may also wish to photograph our friends in the Chevette."

A few yards from our parking space were several park benches. We selected one with a clear view across the bay to the parking lot near the bridge.

We had only been seated a few seconds, and I had barely had time to load the film, when Augustus elbowed me to indicate the arrival of the white Chevette.

"Just as I expected," he chuckled, peering through the binoculars. "They must have thought their compass had blown a fuse."

I raised the camera to my face and clicked the shutter as the skier waved to what he thought were the new scientists standing in front of their car. He pulled the transmitter from his vest, and waved it above his head. The man and woman were gesturing wildly as the skier passed close to their position onshore. The skier waved back to them as he tossed the beeper out into the water.

"Beautiful," I laughed, as I snapped another picture.

"I thought you should enjoy it," Augustus said.

The sun was low in the sky behind us, but Augustus and I were in high spirits as we drove back toward North Park. We had just turned off the freeway when he motioned to the rearview mirror. What I saw when I turned around made my heart stop.

"Who is it?" Augustus asked.

"Previt," I said. A black Porsche was tailgating us. "You'll never lose him in a Buick."

Augustus wrinkled his brow.

"I do not intend to lose him yet," he said. "I have an idea.

He drove down the street at a steady speed of thirty-five miles per hour. Pulling the camera out of my hands, he fumbled with it a few seconds, dropped it in his lap, and lowered the electric window.

"Take the wheel," he ordered.

I put one hand on the wheel to hold the car's direction in line. Augustus thrust his head out the window and looked directly back at the Porsche. Without moving his head, he grabbed the camera from his lap. Just as the Porsche was at its closest position against our bumper, Augustus let fly with the camera, sending it crashing into the windshield of the Porsche. Previt swerved the car onto the shoulder and stopped. Augustus recaptured the steering wheel and sped away.

"Nice work," I said, patting him on the back.

"My pleasure," Augustus beamed. "Sorry about your camera."

"That's okay," I said. "But I wish you could have removed the film. Those pictures were priceless."

Augustus reached under his seat with one hand and held his brown fist in front of my eyes. He opened his fingers slowly for dramatic effect. In the palm of his hand was an orange-and-black roll of Kodak film.

"They're screwing with us," the blonde said.
"Yeah, and I don't like it," the other man answered. He slammed the door and backed the green Dodge away from the Chevette.

When we returned to the Safeway parking lot, Augustus suggested that I buy a late edition of the *San Diego Tribune* and meet him back at the house. I watched him drive away in Hazel's Studebaker.

When I drove up to the house he was waiting for me.

"Park in the backyard," he shouted. "No need to park on the street where someone could recognize the car."

I nodded and proceeded around to the back of the house. Hazel waved hello from the kitchen as I walked up the steps to the back porch. Just as I was opening the porch door I heard a low scream. Hazel and I ran into the living room.

Augustus was pulling Spike off the back of his neck. Spike saw me, jumped to the floor, and began strutting back and forth between my legs.

"No wonder the burglar ran away," Augustus muttered. "Damn cat scared the bloody hell out of me."

"Augustus!" Hazel cautioned. "Watch your language in this house!"
"Sorry, Mum."

Augustus led the way to the basement, with Spike nipping at his shoestrings. He sat at a small work desk and motioned for me to sit beside him. Spike heard Hazel rattle a few pans in the kitchen and flew up the stairs to join her. I took out the newspaper and found the obituary column.

SHEILA SIMMONS
Friends of Sheila Simmons, who was killed in a traffic accident Saturday afternoon, have announced a memorial service to be held at the Himalayan Peace Society Temple, Highway 101 in Encinitas tomorrow at ten o'clock a.m. All who knew Sheila are urged to attend to honor her memory.

"Sheila didn't seem the type to be involved in Eastern religion," I wondered aloud. "Maybe Penny set this up. She seemed like more of a free spirit."
"In any event," Augustus said, "our attendance is required at that service. Or at least within eyesight and earshot of that service."
"What do you mean by that?"
"Well," he said, pouting just a bit while his eyes twinkled, "you are a photographer. Am I not correct?"
"An amateur photographer," I said.

"But capable enough to understand the equipment and compose a decent telephoto picture."

"Yes." I smiled, thinking of the shot I had just taken of the water-skier. "But for some reason, I seem to remember my camera and telephoto lens disappearing into the windshield of a Porsche."

Augustus continued, unfazed by my remark. "You remember the work I used to do with big ear listening devices?"

"Yeah," I answered. "You used to claim you could put together a better system using pipes."

"That was no mere claim," he said firmly, "although I never had an adequate chance to test my work."

"So, get to the point."

"I purchased a big ear at Cal Tech to compare with my pipe system. I improved both systems by adding a set of amplifiers and filters. Do you wish to examine them?"

"You mind telling me first where all this is leading?"

Augustus sighed. "Always the barrister, aren't you?"

Hazel called us to dinner. We postponed the visit to Augustus's equipment closet while we went upstairs to the dining room. Hazel had laid out a feast of rare roast beef with gravy, glistening corn on the cob, a creamy broccoli-and-cheese casserole, and homemade biscuits.

"Spice tea is in the kettle," she said to me as we took our seats at the table. "Help yourself to whatever you want. There is plenty more in the kitchen."

"More?" I laughed.

Augustus and I were eating instead of talking for the next fifteen minutes, although Hazel wanted to know all about our day. Augustus filled her with half-truths about how we had spent the day practicing photography. He told her we had had such a fine time that we were planning to go out again tomorrow.

"I shall finally have the chance to use that wonderful camera you bought me, Mum," he concluded.

"Oh, how wonderful," she beamed. "I was worried you didn't like it."

After dinner Augustus and I helped with the dishes while Hazel fed the cats.

"Spike has behaved herself nicely all day, haven't you Spike." Hazel poured a small cup of warm goat's milk over Spike's cat chow. "Stop treating her so well," I said. "I won't be able to get her home." Hazel kept pouring. "Well, that would be all right with us, wouldn't it, Spike?"

Spike was too busy lapping up the milk to give an intelligent answer.

When Augustus and I returned to the basement, he opened the closet, revealing an array of devices. Some were familiar to me; others were strange and exotic. The largest item was the big ear. He lifted it out of the closet and set it near the work bench where we had been sitting. Then he reached up to the top shelf and handed me a camera fitted with a long lens.

"Hazel bought you a Leica?"

I gazed at it in admiration. It was a far better camera than the one I had lost.

"Mum's friends have good taste," Augustus replied. "That is probably the finest camera on the market."

"She must have paid a fortune," I agreed.

"She got it at a garage sale from some woman whose husband had died," he said.

"Unbelievable."

"You would have a bloody difficult time finding that teleconverter in a camera store."

"What does it do?" I asked.

"It turns that two-hundred-millimeter lens into a six-hundred-millimeter lens," he said. "That translates to a magnification level of about twelve times normal size."

"But it's so small . . ."

"If you find that impressive," Augustus said, placing his hand on the big ear, "this device can amplify sound one hundred times its normal loudness. We should be well equipped for tomorrow."

"Mind telling me what you have planned for us?"

"Not at all," he said. "We get up early, establish ourselves in a place where we cannot be seen, and watch the people who come to the memorial service. We photograph some people; tape some conversations. If the coast is clear, you interview Sheila's friends."

"Why me?" I asked. He did not look up.

"Because, my dear Michael," he said, adjusting a knob on the big ear, "you are Caucasian."

Chapter VII

Tuesday morning was colder than a tin toilet seat, and a ceiling of low clouds spewed angry bursts of drizzle and wind on our heads. Augustus wanted to drive, so I gave him the keys to the Buick. I was glad he hadn't insisted on taking Hazel's Studebaker. The tires were worn and the windshield wipers didn't work.

The fog didn't hit us 'til we were halfway to Encinitas. Augustus steered with his nose up close to the windshield, feeling his way along the coast road like a blind turtle. Then, all at once, the white stucco walls of the Himalayan Peace Society loomed in front of us. I knew from driving past it a number of times that the walls surrounded about twenty acres of open land on a cliff above the beach. A giant arch sheltered two wooden gates at the main entrance. Minarets crowned the wall at various intervals, and lent the property an East Indian appearance, making me feel like I was about to enter the Taj Mahal. And I wasn't far off. A hundred yards behind the main gate the bulbed spires of a temple peered at me through the fog like sentinels wearing turbans.

It was nearly nine o'clock. We had an hour to kill before the start of the memorial service. Augustus found a parking space hidden behind a dumpster a few blocks to the north. Then, clad in rain gear and lugging our equipment, we backtracked to the temple. Neither of us had ever been this close to the place before, but we could tell from the seven-foot wall and locked gates that visitors were not always welcome. The only nice thing about the rain was that it masked the sound of our movements and reduced the risk of our being seen.

There were no safe places along the northern wall. Too many neighbors with big windows. The eastern boundary was out of the question because it ran along the Coast Highway. The western side, though unwalled, was too treacherous to negotiate in the rain because it ran along the slippery cliffs above the ocean. Searching the southern wall, we found a suitable spot where a Mediterranean cypress grew just inside the southeast corner.

Augustus set the big ear on the ground next to the wall. He had covered the contraption with a plastic trash bag for protection against the rain.

"I shall help you up and then hand you the big ear," he said. "Afterward, you can give me a hand."

He cupped his fingers into a stirrup and gave me just enough of a boost so that I could grab the top of the wall and pull myself into a straddling position. Then he handed me the big ear, which I balanced between two branches of the cypress tree.

I surveyed our location. From the standpoint of the temple itself, the Coast Highway, and persons entering the main gate, we were well hidden behind the cypress. But anyone walking outside the property along the wall would notice us easily.

Grabbing a large branch for support, I leaned over and offered my right hand to Augustus. The weight of his two hundred fifty pounds nearly tore my arm out of its socket, but he managed to flop his free hand over the wall and pull himself up to the top. He was panting heavily, but concentrated immediately on the contents of his knapsack, which he arranged along the wall, one item at a time.

Glumly, I examined the photographic equipment I had packed inside my own knapsack. To operate the camera, I would have to look through the foggy viewfinder, focus, adjust the f-stop ring, and squeeze the shutter—all from outside a clear plastic bag, which I had wrapped around the camera to keep out the rain. I decided to solve the problem by prefocusing on the front doors of the temple and by setting the f-stop ring for the gloomy conditions. If the weather changed dramatically, though, I would be out of luck.

Meanwhile, Augustus had his own problems. The big ear was at least three feet tall. There were wires connecting it to a pair of headphones, and then to an amplifier, a car battery, and a tape recorder. All in all he had brought thirty pounds of bulky equipment, with no stable place to put it. Not only was the rain a problem with the electrical hookups, the wind kept shifting the direction in which the ear was pointed.

Every few minutes Augustus would mutter about the impossibility of testing the equipment without a sound source.

"The only thing making any noise out here is the rain," he would say. "How the deuce can I focus on that?"

Both of us were shivering like wet Chihuahuas, and with every gust of wind some piece of equipment would shift, or start to slip off its perch, and I would have to risk falling myself to rescue it.

At about nine-thirty, Augustus startled me with a loud whisper.

"Michael! Look!"

On the Coast Highway, crawling past the main entrance, was the white Chevette. It continued a block or two up the street and disappeared in the fog.

"What do you suppose they're looking for?" I wondered out loud.

"You," Augustus answered quickly. "Did you get a picture?"

"No," I replied, feeling stupid, "I was too shocked."

"Well pull yourself together. We could have used that license number."

The fog deepened. By the time the gates were opened at nine forty-five we could barely see the form of the man who opened them, and the temple itself was now completely invisible. A few people had begun to arrive, but I was too far away to recognize any of them through the mist.

"This is no good," I whispered. "I've got to get closer."

"Forget it," Augustus snapped back. "If anyone sees you, all our efforts will be spoiled. Remember, the chaps in the white car are around here somewhere."

"Don't worry," I said, sliding forward off the wall. "I don't plan to be seen." I jumped down to the wet grass before Augustus had a chance to stop me.

I tiptoed quietly around the base of the cypress tree, still carrying the camera under my arm. When I could see the front door of the temple, I veered away from it, heading toward the back of the building. In a few minutes I found what I was looking for. There was a back entrance to the temple.

I tested the knob and the door opened easily in front of me. A dark hallway led to the dim light of a small room. I crept toward it until I saw another doorway, this one leading into the main hall of the temple. I approached it and peered inside.

About a dozen people were seated on the floor in front of a statue of a giant golden goddess with multiple arms and legs. Bouquets of flowers were nestled around her on the floor. The room was lit by a single spotlight aimed at the statue, which reflected an eerie yellow glow on the faces of the seated visitors. I recognized Penny Boykins seated next to the police detective who had questioned me at Sheila's office. Next to him was the younger policeman I had seen with the detective. I didn't recognize any of the other guests.

The contrast between the glare of the spotlight and the shadowy area where I was standing gave me a false sense of security. As I raised the camera to photograph the mourners an abrupt voice startled me from behind.

"What are you doing here?" The voice belonged to a small, dark-skinned priest wearing a white linen robe. I lowered the camera quickly and donned my ignorant-southern-boy face.

"Ain't it jest awful about Sheila?" I drawled.

The priest pointed to the back door through which I had entered.

"No one is permitted here," he said.

"Just one picture?" I begged. "Her grammaw will want to know who came to the funeral."

The priest's expression did not change.

"You must leave immediately and enter through the main entrance. And you will leave your camera outside."

I retreated, holding my arms up in a gesture of surrender.

When I stepped outside, the fog was clearing in places, but the wind and drizzle persisted. As I rounded the corner of the temple the lens of the camera blew apart at about the same time as I heard a loud pop like a firecracker. The camera was knocked from my fingers and fell to the grass. I was stunned for a second. Then I saw him—Charles Previt—running toward me with a pistol aimed right at my face. The wings of his tailored jacket flapped in the wind as he ran.

I bolted for the ocean, darting back and forth to present a more difficult target. Crack! Crack! Two more shots rang out, one whizzing past my ear as I reached the cliff.

The rocks were wet and treacherous, diving more than one hundred yards to the beach below. I had no choice. Finding a small erosion gully, I jumped forward and began sliding and tumbling down the rock wall. Whap! Another shot struck the mud near my fingers.

My body was gathering speed and I was out of control. Near the bottom of the cliff the gully suddenly ended and I was thrown feetfirst into the air. I fell the final twenty feet to the wet sand, landing heavily on my right ankle. I felt the tendons snap. Knives of pain wracked my lower leg as I tried to struggle forward. At first my leg would not hold any weight, but the sharp crack of another shot, this time stinging the skin of my left wrist, sent me limping forward on sheer adrenaline.

I was able to glance back quickly as I stumbled away from the rocks, clutching my left wrist. Previt was standing at the top of the cliff, barely visible through the low clouds. He hadn't tried to follow me down. Beside him was another man, also dressed in a business suit. I was too far away to make out his face.

Although I had managed to elude Previt temporarily, I was now all but trapped on the beach. The cliffs, slick and dangerous even in the driest of weather, would be impossible to climb in the rain, even if I were completely fit. I had no choice but to keep moving down the beach.

After twenty minutes of painful hobbling—stopping every few steps to catch my breath and rest my injured leg—I noticed that the fog had deepened and I could no longer see the tops of the cliffs at all. Beside me, the breakers had disappeared. I would have to rely on their sound to guide me as I headed south.

I tried to concentrate on the feel of the cool spray against my face as I stumbled along, but the pain in my wrist and ankle was overwhelming. I tried distracting myself with strategies: I knew the cliffs ended at a campground. Previt would also know that. I asked myself what I would do if I were in his place. He had seen me limping after my fall to the sand. Therefore, he knew that I couldn't backtrack to the north, where the cliffs were even more treacherous. My only option was to head south, and he knew it.

The fog presented him with a complicating factor, though. If I could manage to reach the campground first, I could lose myself among the tents and campers. I might even persuade someone to help me.

The campground was less than a mile from the temple and Previt had the advantage of a car. My only hope was that the fog would slow him up enough to give me time to reach the campground. If I encountered Previt or his companion along the way, I planned to head for the breakers and dive underwater. I had grown up around the ocean and I could depend on the breakers to shield me for a time. But Previt would know that I couldn't stay out there forever.

The fog cleared enough for me to see that I was approaching the campground. My right ankle was numb and swollen tight against the inside of my shoe. My wrist dripped fresh blood with every lurch of my body. I felt faint from the shock of my injuries, but the moist breeze in my face kept me awake.

I could just make out the outline of a tent a few yards to my left when the large figure of a man suddenly appeared in front of me. I lunged toward the ocean and was about to throw myself in the water when I heard the man whisper.

"Michael!"

"Augustus, is that you?" I cried.

"Yes," he whispered. "Keep your voice down. The auto is over here." He motioned toward a dark shape near the tent. He came over to my side and hooked his arm under mine, allowing me to lean against him as I hopped on one leg toward the car.

"Previt's nearby," I whispered. "How'd you know where to find me?"

"Please be quiet and get in the auto. We can talk about it later."

Augustus helped me into the front seat and started the car. A gunshot shattered the passenger window behind me.

"Get us out of here!" I shouted, but Augustus had already floored the accelerator.

"Duck!" he yelled as another gunshot smacked the dashboard. The Buick spun through the sand toward the road. I crouched down in the seat and tried to look behind us, but I could see nothing but fog. Augustus spun the car onto the coast road and headed back toward the temple, speeding blindly.

"Where the hell are you going?" I shouted. "Previt's friend might be up there!"

"No," he replied calmly. "I saw them both at the campground."

I was thankful Augustus had driven us to the temple that morning. Otherwise, I would have been stranded on the beach with a set of useless car keys and Augustus would have been stranded near the temple with a useless car. We passed by the front of the temple again and cruised through the town of Encinitas.

"Okay, Augustus," I said. "How did you know where to find me?"

"The big ear," he replied with a toothy grin. "It was superb."

"What do you mean 'superb'?" I asked, incredulously. "Nothing works that far away. Besides, I went down a cliff. You couldn't possibly have heard me."

"Why must you assume I was listening to you?" he said with a smirk.

"Who the hell else would you be listening to?"

Augustus chuckled, thoroughly enjoying my state of confusion.

"After you jumped off the wall," he said, "I saw two men follow you around to the back, so I decided to listen to them. I picked up a gunshot, then some running footsteps, then several more shots. I was quite worried about you."

Our rate of speed was decreasing as Augustus talked.

"After a few moments of garbled noise I could hear the men talking. One of them said you were headed south. The other man said there was a campground down the beach. I heard footsteps running. I deduced they were running to their automobile, so I ran to get ours. Fortunately, I had parked several blocks closer to the temple then they had. I was able to blend in with the campers before they arrived."

"Augustus," I said nervously, as he drove slowly through town. "Don't you think we ought to be moving a little faster? After all, they were right behind us back there."

Augustus laughed. "No problem," he said. "I put sand in their petrol."

Despite the pain of my injuries I was able to laugh as he turned east on Encinitas Boulevard toward the freeway. Suddenly, his smile disappeared.

"We appear to have company," he said.

I turned in my seat and looked behind us. A green sedan was following from a distance of about three blocks.

"I picked it up at the temple," he said. "I shall attempt to lose it."

Augustus pulled onto the freeway and accelerated slowly, moving across three lanes into the fast lane. The green sedan followed, giving us plenty of distance. After less than a mile the exit sign for Santa Fe Drive appeared in front of us. Augustus gunned the accelerator, yanking the wheel sharply to the right as he shot forward, barely missing a small car and a pickup truck, and crossed all three lanes in time to exit. The green car swerved around traffic but managed to pull off the road behind us.

"I thought you said you poured sand in their gas tank," I said, without taking my eyes off our pursuer.

"I did," said Augustus. "That is not Mr. Previt's auto. He was driving the same black Porsche with a broken windshield."

"You suppose he radioed ahead to the green car when we got away?" I kept examining the car to see if I recognized it. I was wishing I had not dropped the camera.

"I doubt it. The auto has no communication antenna. And there was no antenna on the Porsche. I would have noticed."

I gazed back at the car. Augustus was right. The only antenna was the standard AM-FM radio antenna. At the end of the exit ramp Augustus ignored the stop sign and sped onto the entrance ramp again. This time the green sedan was slowed by a large tractor-trailer turning onto the freeway behind us. Augustus used the opportunity to pull away.

I watched the speedometer shoot forward. He leveled off at eighty miles per hour, shifting from lane to lane to pass the slower traffic. Wind was roaring through the broken glass where the bullets had entered the window behind me.

"We have lost it," Augustus shouted above the wind noise.

"Any idea who it was?" I asked.

Augustus shook his head. "I was hoping *you* could tell *me*."

He swerved off the freeway at the Del Mar racetrack and turned onto a side street. He careened around corners first to the left, then to the right, losing us among the exclusive homes of Del Mar Heights. He screeched to a halt near a vacant lot with a panoramic view toward the temple.

"Almost forgot something," he said, opening the door. Ducking down, he worked his way around the car as if checking the tires. Then he got back in the car.

"No transmitters this time," he said. "We are safe now."

From our vantage point we could see all the main roads to the north. There was no car resembling the green sedan.

"It is time we went home," Augustus said. "We must tend to your arm." Blood from my wrist was dripping on the car seat.

"Besides," he said, "there is a tape recording you must hear."

"What recording is that?" I asked.

"Have you forgotten already?" he chided. "I had the ear connected to a tape recorder."

"So?"

"I was hoping you could identify Mr. Previt's friend."

Chapter VIII

Augustus helped me up the back steps and down the hallway to the guest bedroom. Hazel had left a note saying she was out shopping for groceries, and I was thankful we wouldn't have to explain my condition to her. I was exhausted, but my wound wasn't serious. The bullet had burned a shallow streak on my left wrist—more like a scrape than anything else. Augustus found some alcohol, gauze, and adhesive, and in a few minutes I had cleaned the wound and dressed it with a simple bandage.

My ankle was a different story. By the time Augustus had helped me onto the bed, I was completely unable to walk. When I removed my right shoe and sock I saw a purple globe of skin where my ankle had been. I eased both legs onto the comforter and settled my head into the down pillow. I had planned to lie down for only a few moments, but I was soon fast asleep.

Hazel woke me up sometime later, clattering a tray into the bedroom. She set the tray on the bedside table next to me and turned on the lamp. It was seven-thirty.

"Is it really that late?" I asked. "I must have slept all afternoon."

Hazel smiled. "The sleep was good for you. Here, I made you some soup with fresh vegetables."

I could see chunks of red tomatoes and green cabbage as she ladled a generous helping into a china soup bowl. Spike, who had been waiting in the doorway, sprang onto the bed next to me for a better view of the food. I stroked her fur as Hazel poured me a cup of lemon tea.

"Augustus says you're feeling bad because the camera hit the rocks when you fell. Now don't worry about any of that. That was just an old camera I picked up at a garage sale for Augustus. He never even looked at it twice."

I rose as best I could to a sitting position, keeping my right leg straight and raising the pillow behind me to support my back.

"That's very sweet of you, Hazel, but that was no cheap camera."

I took the tray from her as she lifted Spike away from the soup.

"As I was saying, I bought it at a garage sale," she said with an impish grin. "The poor woman who sold it to me didn't know what she had. To be perfectly honest, I didn't know either, except that the gentleman escorting me insisted I buy it.''

I tasted a spoonful of the soup. It was another of Hazel's masterpieces: tangy and flavorful without too much spice.

"This is good," I said.

Spike was purring contentedly as Hazel stroked her behind the ears.

"Just call me if you need anything at all," she said as she walked back to the door. "I'll be right down the hall."

"Thanks, Hazel."

I finished the soup and lifted the china cup full of lemon tea. I had just plopped two lumps of sugar into it when Augustus's tall frame darkened the doorway.

"How is my favorite photographer?" he said, grinning. He was carrying a black box and several photographs.

"I feel a little overexposed," I said. "What have you got there?"

"Evidence," he said. "I have been working in the darkroom while you were enjoying a life of leisure."

Augustus handed me three color prints. I recognized the first print as the one I had taken of the water-skier raising the transmitter high in the air. The second print showed the skier tossing it into the water. The third one was the most interesting. It showed a dark-haired man with a blonde woman standing near the water. The man looked familiar.

"I think I saw this man in Sheila's office with the detective. He was also at the funeral today in the temple," I said. "He was wearing a police uniform and he was sitting between Penny Boykins and the detective."

"Just what we need," Augustus muttered. "The police on Previt's side."

"I wouldn't worry about them," I said. "Penny was the one who told the police about me. She probably thinks I killed Sheila. It makes sense that the police would be trying to find me."

Augustus took one of the prints from my hands. "You are forgetting something."

"What's that?" I asked.

"The man and woman in this photograph were driving a white Chevette. Am I not correct?"

"Correct."

"And you later saw the man in a police uniform?"

"That's right. So what?"

"So, a white Chevette is what you saw the night the man broke into your room. There is a high probability that the man in the photograph is the one who fired the shot at you."

"So far you're not telling me anything I don't already know."

Augustus leaned over and pointed his finger at my chest.

"Since when do the police break into motel rooms without warning, shoot at unarmed people, and run away?"

Augustus had a point.

"Then what's the police connection? Why would a cop act that way?"

"That is a puzzle I have yet to solve. Meanwhile, here."

He handed me the black box. "Use the headphones so Mum cannot hear it."

The box was a small tape player. I put the headphones on and pressed the play button. I heard the sound of rain and footsteps followed by a few seconds of just the rain again. Then there were more footsteps, this time running and splashing. I looked up at Augustus.

"Keep listening," he said.

There were shouts and gunshots, some chaotic rustling noises, and more rain. Finally, I could make out the sound of voices.

"That's him, I think I got him with that last shot." I recognized the voice of Charles Previt.

"He's heading south toward the campground. If we hurry we can beat him there in the car."

This last remark was followed by more footsteps, then silence again. I pressed the rewind button just enough to hear the second voice again.

"No doubt about it," I said. "That's Bob Goren, the president of Argotech."

Augustus sat down next to my good ankle.

"The way I see it," he began, "we have to get more evidence on Previt and Goren. Then we have to find someone outside the police department to show it to."

"How about the U.S. attorney?"

"Who's that?" he asked.

"The federal prosecutor. This is a federal matter because it involves defense money. Besides, the

Feds are better equipped to handle complex cases like this. . . . But how are we going to get more evidence?"

Augustus patted his fingers on the tape player and the photographs.

"The same way we got this stuff."

"You're forgetting," I said, "that I'm not quite up to jogging on the beach just yet. In fact, I'm not sure I'll feel like getting shot at again even when I'm healthy."

"What are you planning to do then," Augustus continued without sympathy, "stay here forever? Not that Mum and I would mind. You're quite welcome, you know. But at the moment you have no job, no place to go, and you are being pursued by a pair of hostile executives who know your face and your automobile, and who apparently have some aversion to your continued existence."

Augustus had a way with words.

"I could always go back to Ocracoke," I said, thinking of the safety of my home and family.

Augustus shook his head and sighed.

"Do you really think that would stop Previt and Goren?"

He was right again. If I left town now I would spend the future looking over my shoulder.

"Okay, you win. What do you propose?"

"I suggest we drive Mum's car to Argotech, and get as close as we can to Goren's office."

I shook my head. "Security's too tight during work hours. We'll never be able to set anything up in the employee lot. And besides, folks around the office are starting to wonder where I am. If I suddenly show up tomorrow it'll cause a stir."

"Who said anything about tomorrow?" He raised his eyebrows. "I was thinking about tonight."

"Tonight? But I thought you wanted to listen to Goren and Previt. They don't work nights."

"Michael, really, sometimes I think you have a bad case of tunnel vision. Did it ever occur to you that we could put everything in place tonight, then monitor the conversations tomorrow at a distance?"

"I see it!" shouted the blonde driver.

"Where?" The man craned his neck to look in the direction she was pointing.

"Behind that middle house. You can just see the trunk."

The man was nodding now.

"I think you're right," he said. "Wait here. I'm going up the driveway a few steps to check out the license number."

The blonde kept the engine running while the man jumped out and ran across the street. He came back a few seconds later.

"It's him all right," he said, slamming the door.

The woman put the Chevette in gear and drove away quickly.

"What do we do now?" she asked.

The man stroked his chin. "Turn left here and park. No sense scaring him away like we did last time."

She made a wide turn at the corner and pulled over to the curb.

"Are we just going to sit here and wait?" she asked.

The man was staring down the street in the direction of the driveway.

"That's right," he said.

The blonde looked puzzled. "What are we waiting for?"

The man never took his eyes off the house.

"The right time to move in."

According to the bedside clock it was past one in the morning when Augustus woke me. The soup tray was gone, replaced by a covered container full of chocolate chip cookies. Augustus was carrying a pair of wooden crutches, which he placed on the bed near my feet.

"Where'd you get them?" I asked.

He gestured to me with one finger over his lips, reminding me that Hazel was asleep. I sat up and pulled a white sock over my throbbing right ankle. Then I stood up and grabbed the crutches. Holding one under each armpit, I began the slow process of walking toward the door. With each creak of the hardwood floor under my weight I worried about waking Hazel, but we managed to make it down the hallway and out the back door with a minimum of noise.

The cold night air did wonders to awaken me. Augustus helped me to Hazel's Studebaker and helped me swing my legs into the front seat.

"Where's all the equipment?" I asked.

"In the trunk," Augustus replied. "I prepared everything before I woke you."

"Don't you ever sleep?"

"I shall be fine," he said. "The excitement should keep me awake."

"Wake up!" the man shouted as he shook the woman roughly.

"What is it? What's going on?" She yawned, trying to shake the sleep from her eyes.

"Thompson's leaving," he answered. "Hurry! Get moving before we lose him again."

The blonde started the engine and followed the distant taillights.

Augustus drove the twenty miles to Sorrento Valley in less than thirty minutes. There were few cars out at that hour of the morning, and the Studebaker seemed to hum with anticipation.

"Do you have your wallet?" Augustus asked.

"Sure, why?" I reached in my back pocket and pulled out my wallet.

"I should think your identification card would be necessary to satisfy security."

I was in the process of extracting my I.D. card when I stopped short. "You say you expect us to go *inside* the building? All we need is for some security guard to tell Goren I visited the office tonight."

"You needn't be so worried," Augustus replied calmly. "It is nearly two o'clock in the morning.

The guards who work this late will not be aware that anyone named Goren exists. In fact, I should think Argotech employs an outside security company."

"That hardly makes me feel better."

"Trust me this once, Michael. Night shift security guards have trouble staying awake. They have specific orders for the examination of identification cards. If the card is valid the guard returns to playing solitaire or drinking coffee."

"So what are they going to think when they see you? Do you have an I.D.?"

"It is not important that I enter the building myself. You are quite capable of handling the equipment on your own, if necessary."

I found the prospect of entering Argotech unsettling. A week ago I had been a stable, if not terribly happy, employee. Now my former bosses were trying to kill me.

Augustus took the Sorrento Valley exit and headed west toward the high-tech district, where rows of sterile, one-story office buildings lined the boulevard. When Augustus pulled the Studebaker into the Argotech parking lot the building was completely dark. There was, however, a well-lit guard office close to the street, with a large sign warning "ALL GUESTS MUST REGISTER HERE."

Augustus pulled up to the guardhouse window. A stern-looking man in a blue uniform shined a flashlight into the front seat. I reached across Augustus, flashing my I.D. card.

"You're okay," the guard said. "What about this fellow?"

"He's the repairman for our mainframe computer," I lied. "We need him to fix the system before tomorrow morning."

"Sorry," he snapped, looking at Augustus. "Can't let you in without proper authorization."

"So how are we supposed to get the computer fixed?" I persisted.

"That's not my problem. My orders are not to let anyone in here except employees and people with valid security passes. If you want me to make an exception you'll have to get special clearance."

"And how do we do that?" I asked.

"Hang on a minute," he said. He stepped back inside the guardhouse and began rummaging through a drawer. He pulled out a clipboard. "It says here that for special clearance I'm supposed to call Mr. Charles Previt at one of these numbers."

"Never mind," I said quickly. "I'll do the work myself. Where can we park?"

"Just pull the car up a few feet. You won't be blocking anybody. We don't get many visitors at this hour."

Augustus moved the car far enough from the guard to be out of earshot.

"What the hell do we do now?" I asked quietly.

"Just what you told the man you would do," he replied. "You take some equipment in and then we leave."

"Oh, that's just great, Augustus," I said. "I can hardly manage these crutches, let alone thirty pounds of electronic gear."

"Michael, you underestimate yourself."

He opened the door and walked around to the

trunk. After fumbling around a few seconds he closed the trunk and returned to the front seat. He was holding a cigar box in his right hand.

"Think you can manage this?" He handed me the box.

"What is it?" I asked.

"A remote listening device, of course." Augustus was in one of his righteously impatient moods.

"Why all the wires?"

A number of colored strands were bulging out from under the box lid.

"I thought it would be nice to have a few wires hanging out for the security guard," Augustus said. "In case he doubts your story about fixing the computer."

"So where's the remote listening device?" I had the box lid open and was searching among the wires.

"It's here in my hand," he said, holding up a metal disc the size of a shirt button.

"You expect me to go inside and plant that thing in Goren's office?" I asked nervously.

"Yes. Unless you have a better suggestion."

He handed me the bug.

"Where should I put it?" I rolled it around in my fingers and dropped it in the box.

"Hide it where it will not be found for at least a month. And remember to wipe your fingerprints off anything you touch in Goren's office, including the microphone."

I nodded uneasily and opened the car door. The cool night air did nothing to calm my nerves. If anything it made me shiver. I opened the car door and climbed out, squeezing the cigar box between my right arm and crutch. The security guard trotted ahead of me to open the main office door. When I had hobbled through the main entrance the door clanked shut behind me and I was alone in the empty building.

I found a light panel at the end of the main hallway and flipped the switches. The corridor lights on my left flickered on. I walked to the end of the hall, where a receptionist's desk and waiting area guarded the executive suite.

I tried to open Goren's office door. Locked. I wiped the doorknob carefully with my shirttail and swung across the waiting area to Previt's office. This time the doorknob clicked in my hand. I opened the door slowly and switched on the light.

Not much had changed since the last time I had seen Previt's office, two years ago. I hobbled over to his desk, being careful not to touch anything. The most logical spot for the bug was directly under his desktop—but it would be too easy for him to discover it there accidentally. A better idea, I decided, was to hide it behind one of the thick volumes on the shelf beside Previt's desk. I chose an old accounting textbook, one I figured he wouldn't look at.

Remembering Augustus's last warning, I cleaned the fingerprints from the bug and carefully placed it on the bookshelf just behind the textbook. The sound quality would be slightly muffled, but at least the bug would be safe.

Having accomplished my mission, I moved back to the door and used my nose to switch off the light. I wiped off the doorknob with my shirttail, grabbed my crutches, and hopped down the corridor, switching off the lights when I reached the panel. The outside air was cold again as I pushed open the main entrance door.

Augustus was waiting for me outside the car.

"Well?" he asked as I flopped heavily into the front seat.

"Mission accomplished," I smiled, feeling relieved. "But I had to put the bug in Previt's office. Goren's was locked."

I saluted the guard as Augustus backed the Studebaker onto the street.

"Did you remember the fingerprints?" he asked, steering the car toward the freeway entrance ramp.

"Got 'em all," I said quickly. Then, retracing my steps in my mind, I came to an awful realization.

"Augustus. I think we may have to go back."

"You don't mean—"

"Yes," I interrupted. "I forgot the cigar box."

Augustus swung the car around in a wide U-turn. As he finished the turn and headed back toward the office, he had to swerve again to miss a car that had been following us with its lights off. It was a white Chevette.

Chapter IX

Augustus floored the accelerator, but the old car only groaned. As the speedometer slowly approached sixty, the steering wheel developed a violent shimmy, and Augustus was forced to slow down to fifty-five. After making a screeching U-turn the Chevette was behind us again. This time its headlights were on high beam, illuminating everything inside our car.

"Augustus," I said, trying not to sound nervous. "This road dead-ends in about a mile."

"Splendid," he said with a frown. "Any suggestions? This automobile is a candidate for surgery."

I thought for a second.

"Turn into that parking lot by the hedge," I said. "There's an alley behind the buildings. Maybe we can lose them back there."

Augustus swung the car over the curb with a jolt, then raced across the parking lot to the other side. He turned sharply to the right when we reached the alley and began a slalom course around potholes and debris, sometimes steering too sharply for the Studebaker's ancient suspension. Suddenly, a large dog appeared in front of us. Instinctively, Augustus slammed on the brakes and yanked the wheel, sending us careening toward a set of garbage cans. We plowed into them with a loud smash and my body was thrown against the dashboard.

After a few seconds I could still hear the tires spinning with a loud whine, but the front axle was lodged on top of a barrel. We were stuck. I reached over and turned the key to kill the engine. Augustus was staring ahead, as if in shock. His face was bloody from its impact with the steering wheel. I looked behind us. Blackened against the headlights of the Chevette was the outline of a man.

"Get out of the car!" he ordered. "Both of you!"

Augustus and I were still numb from the accident. We opened our doors at about the same time and began to climb out. It was only when I put weight on my crutches that I realized how badly I was hurt. My right shoulder had hit the dashboard and it was now painful for me to hold the rubber support under that armpit. I kept the weight on my left side as best I could. Augustus and I were standing on opposite sides of the car, staring into the headlights behind us.

"Turn around and put your hands up against that wall," the man said. He was aiming a pistol in my direction.

We both turned, but as we approached the wall slowly, Augustus shouted, "Penny Boykins, you must stop this hooligan before he hurts somebody."

"Shut up and put your hands up against the wall!" the man ordered.

I turned slightly toward him, recognizing the policeman I had seen in Sheila's office—the same one who had been seated in the temple next to Penny.

"If I raise my arms I'll drop my crutches," I said.

"Put them up against the wall or I'll shoot them off!" he roared.

"Jim, wait!" the voice of Penny Boykins called from the Chevette.

"Stay in the car!" the man yelled.

I heard the car door open.

"Let's hear what they have to say first," she pleaded.

Her footsteps approached me from behind. I looked over at Augustus's bloody face, managing to catch his eye for a brief moment. He softly whispered "Sh-h-h." The man poked him in the back with the pistol.

"How did you know she was in the car?" he asked.

"Simple deduction," Augustus answered calmly. "Michael saw a blonde in a white Chevette near the Crystal Pier."

"But I'm not blonde," Penny interrupted. "This is a wig."

She lifted the blonde wig, revealing her curly red hair.

"Permit me to finish," Augustus continued. "I was able to observe you myself when you were watching the young water-skier toss your transmitter into the bay."

"You were watching that?" the man asked.

"It was a rare pleasure," Augustus answered. "In any event, I noted that the young woman fit Michael's description of Penny Boykins, except for the blonde hair. Of course, it occurred to me immediately that a wig would be the first element of disguise necessary for a redhead. Later, when Michael told me he had not seen the blonde woman at Ms. Simmons's funeral, but that Ms. Boykins sat next to you, the suggestion of a disguise was confirmed."

"And just who the hell are you?" the man asked.

"My name is Augustus Martin," he replied. "I have known Michael since high school. He was not a very popular fellow. I doubt he could recognize a female, much less kill one."

"Hey, thanks a lot," I muttered.

"So why should we believe anything you say?" Penny asked sharply.

"Consider the facts, Ms. Boykins," Augustus said. "Why would Michael hire Ms. Simmons in order to force her off a bridge? Why make an appointment over the phone? Why meet with her at home?"

Penny was lost in thought.

"Why do you care so much about Sheila all of a sudden?" the man said, turning to me. "Why risk your life like this for somebody you've just met?"

He was still pointing the pistol at me.

"No offense to Sheila," I said, "but I really wasn't risking my life because of her. The problem is I've got nowhere else to go. They ransacked my condo. If I tried to leave town Previt would track me down and kill me sooner or later. My only chance is to put together enough evidence to convict him."

"So who's this guy Previt?"

I shifted uneasily on both crutches. "Didn't Penny tell you about the letter?"

Penny glared at me defiantly.

"That letter didn't say anything," she said, placing her hands on her chubby hips.

I sighed.

"Look, Penny," I said. "The letter is what got Sheila killed."

She stood firm, still glaring at me. "Prove it," she said.

I shook my head in exasperation.

"The letter is a crucial piece of evidence against an officer of my company named Charles Previt. Previt must have discovered that his letter was missing, so he wrote another one for some reason we can't figure out. Sheila was unlucky enough to intercept that second letter at an apartment building on Crown Point Drive just when Previt was coming to pick it up. When he caught her reading it he chased her to the bridge in his Porsche and forced her car over the rail."

"How do you know that?" Penny asked in her bratty tone of voice.

"We've been following the evidence, just like you have," I answered.

"Only we have been doing a better job of it," Augustus piped.

The man lowered his gun. "Okay," he said sheepishly. "I guess we owe you guys an apology. But you've got to admit you've been acting awfully suspicious lately."

"Let's go somewhere where we can talk," I said. "My right side is killing me."

I shifted around on my crutches.

"Okay," the man said. "You name the place."

"How about the Denny's near the Crystal Pier?" Augustus suggested. "The sign said it was open twenty-four hours."

I glanced at my watch. It was nearly three o'clock.

"I know where it is," Penny said. "We'll follow you there."

Augustus surveyed the damage to the Studebaker.

"Looks like the garbage can absorbed most of the impact," he said. "These old cars were built like tanks."

"They could use some seat belts," I said, pointing to the dried blood on Augustus's face.

The man with the mustache was asleep when the phone rang. He pulled the receiver off the hook and dragged it to his ear.

"Is this Mr. Charles Previt?" The voice was unfamiliar.

"Yeah, this is Previt. Who's this?"

Previt moved the phone to his other ear and turned to look at the clock. It was ten minutes past three.

"Sorry to bother you, sir," the voice said. "This is the security guard down at Argotech. The sheet says I'm supposed to call you if I come across anything suspicious."

Previt was wide-awake now. "What have you got?" He could hear the guard's excited breathing.

"Well, sir, maybe it's nothing. You see, I'm supposed to check the interior office once every hour."

"Get to the point," Previt snapped. He pulled himself to a sitting position at the side of the bed.

"Well, sir," the guard said. "I just finished my three o'clock round. Maybe it's nothing, but the computer repairman was just here. He left the box in your office."

Previt stood up next to the bed.

"What computer? What box?" he shouted into the phone. "What are you talking about?"

The guard chose his words carefully. "I'm not exactly sure, Mr. Previt. It's a cigar box full of wires. The man said he was fixing the computer, but he was only inside a few minutes. Like I said, I just found his box in your office."

Previt sat back down. Beads of perspiration began to break on his forehead.

"Did you get the man's name?" he asked. He heard the guard rustling through some papers.

"Yes, sir," the guard said. "The name was Thompson. Michael Thompson. At least that was the name on the I.D. I didn't let the other man in. He didn't have an I.D."

"What other man?"

"The black one. There was a black man driving the car."

Previt wiped his forehead on the pillowcase.

"I see. You did right to call. Keep the cigar box in the guardhouse. If the two men come back, you can give them the box. Don't mention that you called me. Act like nothing happened." *Previt was smiling to himself.*

"Yes, sir," said the guard.

"I must take this machine to the garage tomorrow," Augustus remarked, as he backed the Studebaker away from the spilled garbage. "Maybe I can have it worked on before Hazel notices the damage."

"What are you going to tell her?"

"Oh, fiddle," he said. "I really don't know. Perhaps I shall tell her a hit-and-run driver ran into it last night. She parked it out on the street, you know."

In the middle of the night with no traffic it took less than ten minutes to reach the parking lot at Denny's. Augustus pulled into the parking space next to Penny's Chevette. She jumped out of the car and motioned for Augustus to stay put.

"Let Jim and me get a table first," she said. "I'll go in the ladies' room and bring out some wet paper towels so you can wash your face. They'll never give us a table with you looking like that."

We watched the two of them disappear into the restaurant. In a few minutes Penny returned with the paper towels and began wiping the blood from Augustus's face.

"I'm real sorry," she said, swabbing around the cuts as Augustus winced.

"There's still some stains on your shirt, but there's nothing we can do about that. I think we can go in now."

We followed her into the restaurant and found the booth where the man was waiting.

"My name's Jim Simmons," he said, as the waitress brought coffee. "Sheila and I used to be married. At least that's what the court records say. I moved out two years ago."

I almost choked on a gulp of coffee, remembering Sheila's unflattering comments about her ex-husband, the rookie cop.

"I got tired of Sheila nagging me about never being home," he continued. "I guess she told you I'm a cop. Cops keep strange hours, but I would go out with the other guys even when I had a night off. I knew she was right, but I couldn't give up acting like a bachelor. Anyway, when I heard she was dead I felt all guilty inside. So I called up Penny, and she said Sheila was murdered and she thought she knew who did it. I couldn't help myself. I wanted to get my hands on the guy who killed Sheila."

"So what made you think I did it?"

Penny silenced Jim with a quick touch of her hand.

"I guess I blew it," she said, stopping just long enough to swirl some cream into her already cream-colored coffee. "Hey, it all made sense. Sheila came back after lunch looking like hell. I thought she was going to cry. Then she said she was going to see you that same night."

"Hardly enough evidence to hang someone," I said.

"I guess not," she continued. "But it made me suspicious. And when Jim told me later he talked to you in Sheila's office and then you disappeared, I knew you had to be involved somehow."

I looked at Jim.

"So based on that you decided to break into my motel room and kill me?"

"I didn't want to shoot anybody," he said. "But I had my gun ready in case you tried anything. I didn't realize your friend Gus here was behind the door. The gun went off by accident when he hit my arm. Scared the shit out of me."

Augustus and I looked at each other and laughed.

"My name is Augustus," he said. "And I can assure you that I was not behind the door. That was Michael's cat."

"His what?"

"His cat. You needn't worry, though. Spike will not hold a grudge. She would love to meet you."

"So what do we do now?" Penny asked.

Augustus chuckled. "Michael and I were in the process of bugging Mr. Previt's office when we were rudely interrupted."

"Sorry about that," Jim said. "Maybe we can help."

"I doubt it," Augustus said. "Why don't we all meet here tomorrow afternoon and talk strategy."

"Sounds fine to me," Jim said with a yawn.

We shook hands in the parking lot.

"Good luck tonight," Jim said. "Sure you won't be needing any help?"

We shook hands in the parking lot.

"Good luck tonight," Jim said. "Sure you won't be needing any help?"

"No thanks," I said. "We'll see you tomorrow."

Penny and Jim got in the Chevette and drove off.

"Do I really have to retrieve that cigar box?" I asked, as Augustus held open the car door for me.

"I am afraid we have no choice," Augustus answered.

Chapter X

The security guard didn't seem surprised to see us.

"I figured you boys would be back," he said. "You forgot your box." He held out the cigar box toward Augustus. Augustus passed it to me.

"Thanks," I said through Augustus's window. "Where did I drop it?"

I tried to appear unfazed.

"It was back in one of the offices," said the guard. "You left it on the desk."

I forced a smile. "I thought they kept you out here in the guard office," I said, hoping the small talk would help.

"Nope," the man answered. "Got to make my rounds. Every hour on the hour."

His expression didn't change.

"Well, you saved me a trip," I said.

I waved to the guard as Augustus backed the Studebaker onto the street.

"Think he suspects anything?" I asked after we had reached the freeway.

"That is an open question," Augustus answered thoughtfully. "He gave you the box. On its face that would seem to be a positive sign."

"Yeah. You're right," I said. "He handed it right over."

Augustus shifted out of first gear. "On the other hand, he was thorough enough to remove it from the office. That is a negative sign."

"Why do you say that?" I asked.

The old car was picking up speed.

"Because he must have felt the box did not belong there. Most likely he was planning to report the incident to his superiors."

Augustus guided the car onto the freeway entrance ramp.

"So what do you think?" I asked. His remarks were beginning to worry me.

"It matters very little now," he said. "There is nothing we can do about what he thinks. One interesting fact did come of that conversation, however."

"What's that?"

Augustus eased off the accelerator as our speed approached fifty-five.

"The guard leaves his post every hour," he said.

The telephone by the bed rang again. This time Previt was awake.

"Yeah," he answered tersely.

"It's Farmer, sir, the security guard. They just picked up the box."

Previt nodded and smiled. "Excellent, Mr. Farmer," he said. "Tell your supervisor to report to me tomorrow."

The guard cleared his throat. "Yes, sir."

The eastern sky was streaked with dawn by the time Augustus parked the Studebaker. Half-asleep, we tumbled out of the car and trudged up the walk, my tired arms barely able to control the crutches. Hazel was not awake when Augustus opened the front door, but Spike was.

"Good Lord!" he cried in a harsh whisper as he grabbed Spike off the back of his neck and threw her to the carpet. "Can't you teach him to cut that out?"

"Wouldn't want to," I laughed softly. "And she's a her not a him."

Spike meowed her agreement as Augustus shook his head solemnly and wandered down the hall to his room.

I limped back to the guest room, happy to be rid of the crutches as I leaned them against the wall and sat on the bed. My side ached when I pulled off my shirt and jeans, but the sheets were cool as I slid beneath the covers. I was sound asleep before my head hit the pillow.

I was abruptly awakened by ten pounds of fur flopping on my sore chest. It was Spike, with the face of Augustus grinning down at me from beside my bed.

"There," he said. "Since you like the way this bloody cat falls on people, I thought you should enjoy it once yourself."

"What time is it?" I grumped, stroking Spike.

"Past noon. Mum and I decided to let you sleep. She wanted to fix you lunch but I told her we should be dining with some friends. How do you feel?"

I reached over with my left hand to squeeze the ribs on my right side.

"Sore. Not as sore as last night. How about you?"

"I have felt better but I shall make it."

I dangled my legs over the side of the bed. Spike hopped down to help Hazel in the kitchen.

"Did you tell Hazel about the car?"

"She saw it before I could say anything. She had the police here this morning. I heard her complain to them about hit-and-run drivers."

"I hope they didn't examine the front bumper too closely," I said. "They might discover Hazel's Studebaker got crunched by a hit-and-run trash can."

Augustus shook his head.

"They hardly cared," he said. "They gave Mum about five minutes, mostly out of respect for her age. They have no time for what they term 'fender benders.' Especially when the victim is a 1952 Studebaker."

"I've got a reading over here."

The young man motioned for his boss. Charles Previt watched the two men from the door of his office. *They were technicians sweeping the room with metal detectors. The older man laid his own equipment on the carpet and joined his assistant by the bookcase.*

"Right here." *He handed the sensor to his boss. The older man confirmed the reading.*

"Mind if we move some books?" he asked, turning to Previt.

"Move the fucking wall if you have to," *Previt snapped. "Just find the damned thing."*

The older man lifted a handful of books from the shelf. The metal disc lay gleaming in front of him like a polished quarter. He handed the transmitter to Previt, who walked over to the desk to watch.

"How do you turn it off?" he asked.

The technician shook his head. "They don't build 'em with switches. Just throw it down the toilet."

Previt was examining the bug from all angles. "What if I want to keep it?"

The technician looked up. "Just stuff it in your briefcase," he said. "Whoever put it here won't hear a thing."

Previt picked up the morning newspaper from his desk, wrapped the transmitter inside, and shoved the wad into his briefcase.

"You boys finished?" he asked, walking toward the door.

The technician scratched his head. "I guess you could say so. But I'd think you'd want the receiver too."

Previt's head jerked around. "What receiver?"

The technician stood up beside the desk. "Well, maybe they didn't set it up yet. But that particular bug won't transmit much beyond the walls of this building. Whoever put that thing in your office would have to be listening from somewhere nearby."

The younger man tapped his boss on the shoulder. "Might be a relay somewhere."

The older man nodded. "Yeah. Could be. But it would have to be near the building."

Previt glared at the two men. "What are you talking about? What's a relay?"

The older technician was leaning against the desk. "A receiver with a transmitter. One strong enough to pick up the signal from the bug and send it farther away."

"How far?" Previt asked.

"Ten miles. Twenty. Maybe even fifty. Depends on the equipment. It would have to be something larger than that cigar box you were talking about."

Previt rubbed his forehead. "The guard said they both wanted to come in," he thought out loud. "Thompson was on crutches."

The technicians began packing their equipment. Previt looked up.

"When you go out to your truck," he said, "tell the security guard I'm ready to see him now."

Penny and Jim were waiting for us outside the restaurant when we drove up shortly after two o'clock.

"So how are my fellow burglars this afternoon?" Jim asked.

"A little sore, thanks to you and Penny," I complained.

"We figured you might be," he said. "So Penny and I bought you guys a present to make up for the accident." He motioned across the car to Penny.

She pulled a textbook from her purse and handed it to Augustus. He took one look at the cover and began to laugh as he read out loud, *"The Student Driver's Handbook."*

I was the only one who ordered a full meal when we sat down in the restaurant. The others had coffee.

"Sorry, guys," I said, "but I'm starving."

Penny and Jim just smiled. We were all feeling good about each other. Comrades-in-arms.

"Before we get started," Augustus murmured, "do either of you know anything about a green car? A late-model Ford or Chrysler sedan?"

Penny and Jim looked at each other awkwardly, shook their heads, and looked back at Augustus.

"Doesn't sound familiar," Jim said. "Why do you ask?"

"It followed us from the temple yesterday. We managed to lose it on the freeway."

"What about Previt?" Penny asked.

"He drives a black Porsche," I said, watching their faces.

"Don't you think it's one of Previt's people?" she insisted.

"Possibly." Augustus picked up a packet of sugar in his large hand and began toying with it.

"But I have a feeling there are other players in this game."

The conversation was interrupted while the waitress brought my chicken-fried steak special with mashed potatoes and string beans.

"Like who?" Jim asked when the waitress had gone.

Augustus shrugged. "Nothing concrete. Just a feeling."

I took my knife and slathered a pat of butter across my potatoes.

"So what's the plan for tonight?" Jim asked.

Augustus tore the sugar packet and poured some in his coffee. "We need to plant a transmitter near the Argotech headquarters," he said.

I was listening with one ear, but most of my attention was on the chicken-fried steak.

"Why can't we just use the bug you and Mike planted last night?" Penny asked.

"Placing the microphone was the easy task." Augustus winked at mc. "The difficult part is recording the signal. The transmission will not carry more than about two hundred feet."

"So why don't we find a spot two hundred feet away and record Previt's conversations?" Jim asked.

"Because two hundred feet from Previt's office doesn't get us past the guardhouse," Augustus replied. "If the security guard had let me go in last night with Michael, I would have carried a relay transmitter and battery. We could have found a decent spot in Michael's office to hide it. The relay I have in mind has a range of over fifteen miles, which should allow us to record Mr. Previt from my home in North Park."

Jim was listening intently.

"But won't the guard be suspicious if he sees you again?" he asked.

Augustus nodded. "That's where you and Penny come in," he said. "I'll give you the details when we meet tonight."

"Are you sure the plan will work?" Penny asked nervously.

I looked up from my green beans. Augustus had a strange look on his face.

"In this case I would say the possibilities are against us," he answered.

"If it doesn't work," Jim said, "we won't be bugging any buildings for a long time. I don't have to tell you guys that all this bugging shit is illegal as hell."

"Yes, sir?"

The security supervisor stood at the door. Previt looked up from his desk and motioned the man into his office.

"The guard saw nothing larger than a cigar box," Previt said. "Am I right?"

The supervisor nodded. "That's what he said, sir."

Previt began pacing toward the bookshelf. "I want you to call the agency and arrange for the same man to be on duty tonight."

"No problem, sir. They have Farmer scheduled every night this week."

Previt smiled. "Excellent."

The supervisor rose to leave. "Anything else, sir?"

"Yes, there is one more thing," Previt said. "I want you to alert the police. I expect Mr. Thompson may be returning tonight."

It was well past midnight when Augustus and I drove down the alley with the headlights off, stopping at the same set of garbage cans we had hit the night before. A few minutes later we heard the sound of Penny's Chevette behind us. All four of us got out and stood as a group in the shadows near Penny's car. Augustus had fashioned a walking cane out of aluminum pipes, and I was able to limp around without the hassle of crutches.

"Park on the street as close to the guardhouse as you can," Augustus said, "but keep your automobile hidden. Pull the car onto the curb if you have to. The guard makes his rounds every hour. Stay out of sight until you see him enter the building."

He raised the trunk of the Studebaker and took out a large box full of electronic equipment.

"Here," he said, handing the box to Jim. "I have preset everything except the antenna. Take this to the far end of the parking lot beyond the guardhouse. Remove the components from the box and find a place where you can hide them near the fence. Pull the antenna up as far as it will go and tie it to the fence with this."

He held up a small loop of metal wire.

"Penny," he continued. "Station yourself near the front of the building to watch for the guard.

When you see him coming down the hallway wave to us and we will drive up to distract him. Then wait next to Jim beside the fence. Michael will ask to enter the building."

Penny nodded. "And when Jim and I see the guard walking Mike to the front door, we run like crazy back to my car."

"There you have it," Augustus smiled. "We shall meet again tomorrow at the restaurant. Two o'clock."

Penny and Jim climbed back into the Chevette and drove down the alley, keeping their lights off as a precaution. Augustus and I followed at a distance of a hundred yards. When we were within about a block of the parking lot, Penny guided the Chevette onto the sidewalk and drove along a tall row of shrubbery to within a block of the guardhouse.

Augustus parked on the street well behind her, so that neither car could be seen by the guard. When both cars had parked, we watched Jim creep slowly away from the Chevette to get a better view of the guard.

At a few minutes past one, Jim motioned for Penny to get out of the car. We watched her open the car door and tiptoe out to join him. The two of them walked quickly along the hedge and disappeared around the corner.

Augustus released the parking brake and allowed the Studebaker to coast down the street toward the corner of the hedge where Jim and Penny had disappeared. He stopped when he reached a position where he could watch Penny at the front door. Again we waited.

"I should have told Jim to wear black," Augustus whispered. "He is too prominent in that white shirt." I looked across the parking lot to the corner of the fence. Jim's shirt was the brightest object in the area.

"Too late now," I said quietly. It occurred to me that Jim Simmons was not endowed with an abundance of common sense. Maybe that's why Sheila married him, I thought.

A few seconds later Penny waved to us from her position near the front entrance. Then she ran around the corner to the fence.

"Our cue," Augustus whispered. He started the car engine and switched on the headlights, gunning the motor to make as much noise as possible. He pulled up beside the guardhouse and honked the horn just as the guard was returning to his post. The guard jumped.

"Hey, what's the idea? You boys trying to give me a heart attack?" He looked annoyed.

"Just wanted to make sure you were awake," Augustus quipped. The guard walked up to Augustus's window and stuck his head in.

"And just what do you fellows want tonight?"

I pointed to the front entrance.

"I need some papers," I lied. "Think you could let me in?"

"My pleasure," the guard said.

He walked around to my side of the car and helped me climb out. I followed him toward the main entrance, hoping that Jim and Penny had already escaped.

The guard held the entrance door for me and switched on the hall light. I stalled the guard at the front door by pretending to have trouble with my cane. We were stopped by the sound of sirens screaming behind us. I turned around at about the time two uniformed policemen came racing toward me.

"Up against the wall, buddy!" one of them shouted. The other grabbed my cane and spun me toward the wall, kicking my legs apart and holding my wrists in the air.

"Hey, watch it!" I cried. "That ankle's swollen."

The cop frisked me from top to bottom.

"Cuff him and get him to the car," the other cop said.

The officer grabbed both wrists behind me and applied the steel handcuffs. He jerked my arm to start me toward the patrol car, but my leg would not support the weight. I fell to the asphalt, landing on my sore right side.

"Hey, dumbass," the other cop said. "He can't walk."

The two men each grabbed one of my arms and pulled me to my feet. They half carried me to the car as I hopped on one leg.

As they were shoving me into the back seat, I looked over toward the Studebaker. Augustus was spread-eagled against the side of the car, his palms resting on the roof. The sound of voices caused me to turn back toward the side of the building. Penny and Jim were being led, handcuffed, to a second patrol car. The cop behind them was reading from a small card.

"You have the right to remain silent. Anything you say can and will be used against you in a court of law. . . ."

Chapter XI

Police cars are built for Munchkins. There was no room for me to stretch out my right leg, and my hands were cuffed behind me for the entire trip. I spent thirty minutes shifting my body as best I could, trying to keep my leg from cramping. The cop who had dumped me on the asphalt read me my rights on the way downtown. The driver kept up a constant chatter with the police dispatcher. I understood an occasional "ten four."

When we reached the police station, I was pulled out of the back seat and carried down a hallway to a cell furnished with two flat bunks and an open toilet. Less than five minutes later the cell door was opened and Augustus Martin came tumbling in.

"Plan didn't work," I said, trying to keep a straight face.

"On the contrary," Augustus answered, "the plan worked perfectly, but we were snookered."

He sat beside me on the lower bunk.

"What do you mean, 'snookered'?" I asked.

He lowered his voice.

"Consider the facts. The police came to arrest us before the security guard returned to the booth. That means the police were tipped off before we arrived."

It took me a second to understand what Augustus was saying.

"You mean Previt knew we were coming?" I asked.

Augustus nodded. "It would appear so," he said. "There are a few pieces in this jigsaw puzzle that seem to come from the wrong box. I fear we may have overlooked the obvious."

"Like what?"

"Like the green automobile which followed us from the temple."

"What about it?"

"I saw it on the street as we were leaving the parking lot tonight."

Augustus stood up and began pacing back and forth between the bars and the toilet.

"You saw the detective in the temple, did you not?"

I nodded.

"It may just be," Augustus continued, "that he was a part of our arrest." Augustus stopped pacing and looked straight at me.

"That sounds like good news to me," I said.

He was frowning and pacing again. "Maybe." He rubbed his forehead as if to massage his brain.

"What do you mean, 'maybe'?" I persisted. "Doesn't that mean the police will start cooperating with us now, when they hear our story?"

He sat down next to me and spoke in a whisper.

"There are indications that the detective is not working for the police. At least not on this case."

That frightening possibility had never occurred to me.

"What makes you say that?"

"I can put my hands on nothing tangible. However, I have begun to suspect that we are examining the facts from an improper perspective."

I could tell by the creases in his forehead that he was deep in thought. He was about to speak again when a police sergeant appeared at the cell door. He snapped a key in the lock and motioned for us to follow him.

"You boys are free to leave," he said.

"What's the deal?" I asked. I pulled myself up, using Augustus's shoulder for support.

"Don't ask questions," the sergeant replied, opening the hall door for me as Augustus and I followed a few steps behind him. "Besides, I wouldn't know the answers anyway. When the boss tells me to let people go, I let them go."

"Where's my car?" Augustus asked.

"Right where you left it," the sergeant answered. "There's a taxi waiting outside to take you there. The driver's already been paid." He pointed to an exit at the end of the hall.

We retrieved our personal effects at the front desk and walked outside. The taxi was parked near the door.

"Hey you guys, wait for us!" a female voice cried behind us. It was Penny. She and Jim trotted up to the cab as Augustus helped me into the front seat. She gave Augustus a hug and then leaned in to give me one as well.

"What happened to you guys?" I said. "We didn't see you in there."

"One of the privileges of being a cop," Jim laughed. "Once they recognized me it was easy to explain that we were staking out some suspects at your place of business. I'll probably catch some hell for not going through proper channels, but you guys won't have to worry about being charged with anything. Say, how do you like the cab? Nice touch, huh?"

It should have occurred to me earlier how strange it was for the police to be providing a taxi.

"Thanks, Jim," I said. "I don't think I could stand another ride in the back seat of a police car."

Jim grinned and nodded. "They're not built for comfort, that's for sure."

Penny was tapping on Augustus's arm, trying to get his attention. "So when do we see you guys again?" she asked.

I could tell Augustus enjoyed her feistiness.

"We can meet at my house this time," he said. "If you have some paper I shall give you my address."

The house was quiet when Augustus and I returned. Augustus helped me to my room and said good night as he left. We were both exhausted and my leg hurt. I fell asleep fully clothed on top of the covers.

My dreams were shattered early the next morning by Augustus, who was shaking me violently with both hands. His eyes were wild.

"Michael! Wake up!" It took me a few seconds to shake the sleep out of my head.

"What's the matter?" I sputtered. "What's wrong?"

"I cannot find Mum," he cried. "She is neither in the house nor out in the yard. It is not like her to go off somewhere without telling me."

He was pacing slowly back and forth beside the bed.

"Do you suppose she might have discovered we were missing?" I asked. "Maybe she went out looking for us."

"No," he answered. "She knows I often go out experimenting with my equipment. In any case, she would have left a note."

I sat up. Suddenly, it occurred to me something was missing near my feet.

"Augustus, where's Spike? Did you see her when you were looking for Hazel?"

Augustus shook his head. "No, I must say I was not thinking about cats," he said. "But now that you mention it, I cannot recall her jumping on me when we came home last night."

I scratched my head. "Augustus, do you mind

checking behind the refrigerator? That's where she hides when she's frightened."

Augustus left the room and returned a few moments later, cradling Spike in his arms.

"You had it right," he said. "She was behind the refrigerator, scared to come near me."

He plopped Spike down in my lap. Her heartbeat was racing and she was shivering in spasms.

"Whatever scared her sure did a good job," I said. "I wonder what happened."

Augustus was gone when I looked up. He returned a few minutes later, his brown fingers stained red with blood. His eyes were moist. I thought he was about to cry.

"Augustus," I said. "What is it?"

He sat next to me and put his head in his hands. "The cats," he whispered hoarsely. "When you mentioned Spike, I realized that I had not seen Tigger or Jinx. After I brought Spike to you I went to look in the living room. I found them both lying dead behind the sofa. They were shot in the head."

"Who would kill a cat?" I wondered aloud.

"A sadist," Augustus said, tears forming in his eyes. "Poor Mum."

"We'll find her," I said. "If I have to kill Previt myself, we'll find her." I had never heard myself talk that way before.

Her hands were strapped to the arms of the chair.

"The name of the nigger!" Goren shouted.

Hazel Whittington bit her lip but said nothing. He slapped her red cheek again.

"You can beat me unconscious," she sobbed. "I shall never tell you his name."

Augustus was burying the cats in the backyard when the doorbell rang. Spike tore out of my hands and raced behind the refrigerator.

I limped to the front door and opened it. Penny and Jim stood on the front porch. I led them to the basement, where we seated ourselves in a circle of small work benches. Augustus joined us a few minutes later. Before anyone could say a word, the telephone rang upstairs.

Augustus raced up the steps. A few seconds later he reappeared at the top of the staircase but did not walk down.

"Augustus, what is it?" I asked.

He was lost in thought. "The man identified himself as Charles Previt," Augustus said quietly. "If I wish to see my mother alive I must arrange for Michael Thompson to meet him alone tonight at midnight at the reflecting pool in Balboa Park."

His voice was trancelike.

"Did Hazel say anything?" I asked.

Augustus sighed. "She said I must do as Mr. Previt asks and everything will be all right."

While he was walking aimlessly down the steps, I noticed that Penny was looking at me.

"You're not going to meet him, are you?" she said. "He'll kill you."

I shrugged my shoulders.

"We don't have any choice," I said. "He knows where to find me now. He can come for me any time he wants to."

My words sounded brave, but I was shuddering inside, like Spike.

Augustus reached the bottom of the steps and sat down at his bench.

"We have ten hours before your meeting tonight," he said, controlling his voice. Then, turning to Jim, "You and Penny should survey the area around the reflecting pool. See if there is anywhere you can hide tonight without being seen. Previt will suspect that Michael is bringing friends, so he will move Michael to another spot. You must therefore be prepared to follow quickly—"

Jim interrupted. "And where will you be?" he asked.

"I plan to be very close." Augustus said. He was fighting back tears with all his strength.

"But Previt knows your car," I objected.

Augustus shook his head.

"I shall rent a car for tonight," he said, "but I shall not be sitting in it."

"Where will you be?" Penny asked.

"Not far away," he answered evasively. The room was silent while we all considered the plan. Finally Jim spoke.

"What will you and Mike be doing this afternoon while Penny and I are down at the park?"

Augustus looked up. "I have a few ideas," he said. "But you needn't worry about us. You and Penny will have enough to do."

Jim looked puzzled for a moment, then stood up.

"Well, Penny, I guess it's time we got moving," he said.

Penny followed him to the steps.

"Good luck," I said.

Penny ran over to me and planted a sloppy kiss on my cheek. "You're the one who needs the luck, Mike," she said.

The anchorman led off the news hour.

"A break-in last night at the offices of a Sorrento Valley defense contractor has left company officials wondering why the burglars are out on the street. John Phillips has the story."

The scene shifted to an interviewer in Charles Previt's office.

"I'm here with Charles Previt, chief financial officer of Argotech Enterprises. Mr. Previt, you say this office was burglarized last night by a former employee trying to obtain defense secrets?"

"That's right." *Previt's face looked indignant.*

"How did you find out about the burglary?" the reporter asked.

Previt's eyes glared into the camera. "Our security personnel notified me last night. The police didn't even have the courtesy to phone me."

"And you say the police know who did it?"

Previt gestured impatiently. "Of course they do. The criminals were caught red-handed."

The camera swung to the reporter. "And the burglars were taken to jail?"

The reporter pointed the microphone back at Previt. "That's my understanding. And then I found out this morning that they were released without bail."

The reporter hesitated. "Why would they be released?"

"You know the answer as well as I do," Previt said. "The system is soft on criminals. One of the burglars was a lawyer here at Argotech. He probably started talking about his rights and they let him go." Previt's jaw was firm.

"What do you think the burglars were looking for, Mr. Previt?"

The camera panned around the office.

"Sensitive information," Previt said, holding the metal bug up to the camera. "We found this in my office. Apparently, some group was hoping to record my conversations."

The reporter looked curious. "Who would want that kind of information?"

Previt never flinched. "Enemies of the United States."

The scene shifted back to the anchorman.

"Our latest information indicates that one of the suspects was Michael Thompson, the attorney referred to by Mr. Previt. The other suspects have yet to be identified. The police will not comment on the reason for the suspects' release."

When we were alone again, Augustus pulled a metal contraption from the closet.

"Never thought I would be using this device again," he said. It took me a moment to recognize the old telescopic listening device he had developed in high school.

"You're not planning to go back to Argotech, are you?" I asked.

"Maybe, maybe not," he said. His expression was distant.

"Augustus, what are you talking about?" I asked.

A look of determination came over his face.

"Michael," he said. "Do you know anyone at Argotech who could help us from the inside?"

I thought for a moment. "No," I said. "Everyone I know would either be useless or too close to Previt."

Augustus put his hand on my shoulder.

"Name one," he said.

I thought for a second.

"Well," I said, "Previt's secretary, for instance. Lisa Crenshaw. She's always been real friendly to me, but she's too close to Previt."

"Perfect," Augustus shouted, clapping his hands together.

"What do you mean, 'perfect'?" I said. "She's the last person we need. She's been working for Previt longer than I've been at Argotech."

"And maybe just long enough to see through him," Augustus shot back.

I had never seen him in such a mood.

"No way," I said. "Previt's too smooth. The secretaries love him."

Augustus banged his fist on the pipes.

"Maybe so," he responded. "But we have no other option."

Augustus helped me upstairs to a chair beside the living room phone. I dialed the Argotech number.

"Lisa Crenshaw, please," I said to the switchboard operator.

Augustus took the phone. "Yes," he said. "Is this Ms. Lisa Crenshaw? . . . Excellent. Ms. Crenshaw, I understand you are Mr. Previt's secretary . . ."

He was using his finest British accent.

"Wonderful. . . . You see, my name is George Stapleton from the United Charities of North County. Mr. Previt has been so wonderful to us this year that we wanted to give him an award. A surprise, you know. . . . Yes, that's right. . . . Yes, he is a very nice man. . . . You wouldn't know by chance where he could be reached this afternoon. . . . Oh really? . . . Now that is extremely helpful. . . . Thank you so much for your time. . . . Yes, he should be rather surprised. . . . Be certain not to mention this conversation to him. . . . Yes. . . . We do not want to spoil the surprise. . . . That's right. . . . Thank you. . . . Goodbye." He hung up the phone.

"So what's the story, Mr. Stapleton?" I said.

A faint glimmer stole across his troubled face.

"Previt's having dinner tonight with Goren at the Cardiff Fish House. Lisa made the reservations herself."

In less than an hour after the telephone call, Augustus had driven us to the National Car Rental agency at the airport, where we rented a new Ford Thunderbird to replace Hazel's Studebaker. After loading the sound equipment into the trunk, we were on our way to the beach.

Chapter XII

I was barely able to keep up with Augustus as he marched around the Cardiff Fish House to the beach, looking for the best spot to set up the amplifier. I could negotiate the cane fairly nicely on firm ground, but out there the rubber tip kept sinking into the sand as we walked. I found I could make better time by turning the cane upside down like a walking stick, using the flat metal handle as an extra foot. After a while I got tired of following Augustus and sat down beside some seaweed. Finally he stopped marching around and walked over to where I was resting.

"This will not be easy," he said, his giant body eclipsing the late-afternoon sun.

"What's the problem?" I asked.

Augustus pointed to the fish house.

"You will observe," he began, "that we shall have an unobstructed view of everyone who is dining tonight."

Employees were clearly visible through the giant glass panels, preparing the tables for the evening meal.

"So far no problem," I said.

Augustus sat down beside me.

"On the contrary, that is exactly the problem," he countered. "If we can see into a partially darkened restaurant this easily, think how clearly all the diners will see us."

Once again his logic was unassailable.

"Any ideas?" I asked, digging a trench in the sand with my cane.

"Only one," he said. "We must position the equipment while Previt and Goren are being seated, then we must hide."

The cane was beginning to strike water.

"Won't they see all the equipment?" I asked, scraping at right angles to begin the corner of a moat.

"We can bury most of it under the sand. Only the pipes need be visible. Perhaps we can camouflage them with some seaweed."

I had finished two corners and was heading for the third. My moat was almost complete.

"But if you wait until Goren and Previt get here, you increase the risk of being seen," I observed.

I scraped out the fourth corner and looked with pride upon the foundation of my castle.

"That is a risk we must assume," he said. "Meanwhile, let us bury these wires."

I dragged the cane behind him, expanding my moat into a long trench between the components. Augustus laid the wire along the bottom of the trench and covered it with dry sand. He had rigged the amplifier so that it was powered by a car battery. I dug two large holes into which Augustus placed the amplifier and battery. He placed a cassette recorder on top of the amplifier and plugged it in. Then he found some seaweed to drape across the telescopic pipes.

"Now we wait," he said as he sat down beside me again.

Charles Previt sat on the long couch in Bob Goren's office. Goren left his desk to take a seat in the office chair beside him. They spoke in low voices.

"You think we need to bring her to the park?" Previt asked.

Goren shook his head, "She'd only be in the way."

Previt nodded. "So when do we get rid of her?" he whispered, his dark eyes studying Goren's face.

"We need her alive for a few weeks," Goren said. "Long enough for Thompson to spend money and get his hands dirty."

Previt's expression darkened further. "You're the lawyer," he said. "But I don't like it this way. I won't feel comfortable until they're both dead."

It was after eight o'clock when I noticed an attendant parking Previt's black Porsche beside the restaurant. The sky was darkening rapidly and we were beginning to feel a bit safer.

"They're here," I told Augustus.

A few seconds later I saw the unmistakable profiles of Charles Previt and Bob Goren as they were seated near a corner window.

"Over there," I pointed. "Last table on the right."

Augustus adjusted a pair of headphones over his ears and aimed the pipes in the direction of Previt and Goren. He pushed a switch on the amplifier. The tape wheels inside the cassette player started to turn.

"They're coming in loud and clear," he said, handing me the headphones.

I could hear Previt talking.

"Nice of all these witnesses to see us having a quiet dinner together."

Goren chuckled. The silhouettes of their heads bobbed like marionettes in the candlelight.

Our spying was interrupted by the figure of a middle-aged man racing toward us on the beach. It was the detective. He was dressed in a dark business suit and was kicking up sand with his shiny black shoes as he ran.

"We've got company," I said to Augustus, as I yanked off the headphones and grabbed my cane.

I tried, but there was no way I could run on my bad ankle.

The detective approached to within a few yards and drew a pistol from the pocket of his coat. He gestured with it toward the parking lot. I followed Augustus in the direction the man had indicated. Neither of us said a word as we made our way across the sand.

"Turn left," the man ordered when we had reached the first line of cars. "'Third one down."

A green sedan was parked three cars from the end of the line.

"Get in," the voice ordered again. "Front seat. You drive, big guy."

He tossed the keys to Augustus. I struggled awkwardly into the passenger seat beside Augustus. The man pulled my cane into the back seat after I had closed the door.

"Head out nice and slow," the voice commanded. "We're going to Hotel Circle."

Augustus started the engine and drove us out of the parking lot to the freeway.

On the beach the cassette wheels continued to spin and the volume needle jumped.

"It'll be the easiest three million we ever made," Goren said, laughing.

The sound of wineglasses clinked in the abandoned headphones.

"We'll have to buy the dogs some steak," Previt said.

"Turn in here," the man directed when Augustus had turned into Hotel Circle.

The man leaned over the seat back and pointed in the direction of a Holiday Inn. "Park there," he said. "We'll walk the rest of the way."

Augustus pulled into an open parking space.

"Now get out," the man said. "Walk to the elevator at the side entrance. We're going to room four-seventeen. I'll be right behind you holding a pistol in my coat pocket. First one that opens his mouth around any strangers gets a bullet in the back."

I hobbled behind Augustus as best I could. The thought of the loaded pistol made my gut queasy.

A man and woman with a small boy were waiting at the elevator as we approached.

"We went to Sea World!" the toddler squealed, looking right at me. He held up a stuffed dolphin. I forced a smile, but said nothing, remembering the detective's warning.

The family got off at the third floor. We stayed on to the fourth.

"Down the hall," the man directed.

Once again I followed Augustus. Room 417 was the last door on the left. We reached the locked door and waited for the detective. He stopped about ten feet behind us.

"Open the door," he said, tossing Augustus the room key. Augustus unlocked the door and swung it open.

"Go to the foot of the second bed and sit on the carpet."

Augustus led the way into the room. The window beyond the beds looked out onto the parking lot and the freeway. I laid my cane on the second bed and joined Augustus on the floor.

"Who wants to be first?"

My body froze when I heard the words. I saw the man unsnap a set of handcuffs from his belt.

"You," he said, pointing at me. "Put these on your friend. Nice and slow. One hand at a time."

He dropped the handcuffs in my lap.

"I don't know how they work," I said, staring at them as if they were a pair of Rubik's Cubes.

"You don't need to know," the detective snapped. "Just do as I say."

I looked at Augustus. He held out one wrist toward me. I pressed the metal buckle against his skin. The clamp swung easily across and locked by itself.

"Now run the chain behind the leg of the bed and cuff his other wrist behind his back."

Augustus scrunched down awkwardly against the corner of the bed and held his arms behind his back. I locked the handcuffs, chaining him to the bedframe.

"Now it's your turn."

The man motioned me around to the bedpost next to the window. With his face just a few feet away from mine I could see that he was older than he had appeared at the beach. He must have been close to fifty-five or sixty.

"Turn around," he ordered, pulling my arms behind me. I felt the metal cuffs snap around my wrists. I tried to pull my body forward. I was locked to the bedpost. He pulled the pillowcases off two of the pillows and returned to my end of the bed.

"Just in case you were thinking of making any noise," he said.

He twisted one pillowcase into a gag that he pulled across my mouth and tied tightly behind my head. I watched as he did the same to Augustus.

"Now if you boys will sit tight for twenty-four hours, I'll be back to get you tomorrow."

The room was quiet for a few seconds after he left. I leaned forward toward the window as much as I could—just enough to see the parking lot four stories beneath us. The detective was not alone as he strode rapidly toward the green sedan. Beside him was a tall redhead. As she turned to open the passenger door, I recognized the face of Sheila Simmons.

My heart traded places with my stomach.

Bob Goren typed the final page on the word processor. The document was too sensitive to be seen by a secretary. Previt fidgeted near the office door.

"Can't you hurry up?" he said. It was past ten o'clock at night.

"I'm almost done," Goren answered. "This document is our insurance policy. Once Thompson signs it and spends some money he's one of us."

I was forced to listen to Augustus scraping his handcuffs against the metal bedframe in the dark. Seeing Sheila with our captor had destroyed my incentive. I forgot temporarily that Hazel's life might depend on my making it to the Balboa Park reflecting pool by midnight.

It was more than an hour later that Augustus, with a jolt, had managed to lift his end of the bed enough so that the handcuffs slipped under the bed roller. He stood, still handcuffed behind his back.

Turning his body slightly so that I could see his hands, he motioned toward his mouth with his thumbs. I understood that he wanted me to remove his gag. Unfortunately, my own hands were behind the bedpost against the wall. I shifted my body around as much as I could so that my right hand could touch the top of the mattress.

Augustus lay on the bed and turned the back of his head against my hand so that I could feel the cloth knot. We were both grunting as I tried to untie it. The process was painstakingly slow because Augustus kept shifting his head, unaware that he was moving the knot away from my fingers. When I finally tugged the gag free, Augustus stood up again.

"The gentleman has apparently removed the telephone," he said, "so I must go for help."

I protested with a few loud grunts but he was already standing against the door, twisting the knob behind his back. The chain of the handcuffs clattered against the door. In a few seconds he had disappeared into the hall. The door slammed shut behind him.

He was gone for at least ten minutes, but when he returned his cuffs were missing and he was accompanied by a hotel employee carrying a large toolbox.

"Michael, this is Robert," Augustus said, grinning. "He is the maintenance supervisor."

I grunted a muffled "hi," which came out more like "glp." The man untied my gag quickly.

"Thank God," I said, "I thought I'd never breathe fresh air again."

The man used a wire clipper to free my wrists in a matter of seconds.

"That should do it," he said. "I've seen a lot happen around this hotel but this one takes the cake. Sure you don't want me to call the police?"

Augustus shook his head. "Thank you but no. As I informed you earlier, we shall go to the police ourselves."

The man stuffed his wire clipper back in the toolbox and turned toward the door.

"Well, if they need any witnesses, tell them to call me."

He walked out the door. Augustus smiled at me.

"So now we need yet another auto to return us to the beach," he said.

My mind was elsewhere.

"I saw Sheila," I said vacantly. Augustus sat on the bed across from me.

"I was afraid of that," he said.

My jaw fell open. "You mean it doesn't surprise you that she's alive and working with the man who kidnapped us?"

Augustus inhaled deeply. "I wonder . . .," he said, ignoring my question.

I stood up quickly and grabbed my cane.

"Augustus, we don't have time to think. It's past eleven o'clock. We barely have time to catch a cab to the beach and drive the rental car back to the park."

Augustus was still seated. He had his head in his hands. I thought I heard a slight sniffle.

"Augustus, what is it?" I asked.

"Nothing," he said quietly. "Just thinking about Mum, I guess."

Chapter XIII

It was nearly eleven-thirty by the time the cab brought us back to the Cardiff Fish House. We found the rental car and Augustus drove south again toward Balboa Park. The anxiety of my impending meeting with Previt and the cool night wind from Augustus's open window kept me wide-awake as we drove.

"We shall not have much time when we reach the park," Augustus said, as his shirt collar flapped in the breeze.

"I have the only two transmitters. They are both in the back seat," he said.

The cold air did not seem to phase him, but I was freezing.

"What do you plan to do with them?" I shuddered and rubbed my arms briskly. He didn't take the hint.

"Listen to Mr. Previt, of course."

I reached across Augustus and closed his window.

"Previt's men will be all over the place," I said. "You won't have time to plant bugs."

Augustus rolled the window halfway down again.

"Time is not our problem," he responded. "Previt and Goren cannot afford to hire help. It would mean subjecting themselves to blackmail or betrayal. That is why Previt has been operating alone."

We were approaching the Balboa Park exit.

"What about Sheila and the detective?" I asked.

Augustus turned onto the ramp and headed east toward the park.

"I am only beginning to understand their respective roles," he said. "The only conclusion I have reached is that they are not working for Previt."

I was beginning to shiver.

"How can you be so sure?" I asked. I rolled Augustus's window up again.

"Mr. Previt arranged a meeting tonight with you," he said. "I can think of a number of reasons why he would desire such a meeting."

He lowered the window a crack.

"Such as?"

"Such as attempting to bribe you into silence," Augustus said. "Even a man as cold-blooded as Previt would shrink from the prospect of murder. The ensuing police investigation might jeopardize his embezzlement scheme."

It was ten minutes before midnight.

"So why does that mean Sheila and the detective can't be working for him?"

Augustus sighed impatiently. "Michael, really. Does it seem even remotely reasonable that Previt would kidnap Mum to force you to the park tonight, only to have an assistant lock you in the Holiday Inn?"

I could see the park entrance.

"Maybe they aren't working with Previt," I said. "But they sure as hell aren't working with us. And if you add Penny and Jim to their group, you have four extra people to worry about, besides Previt and Goren."

Augustus shook his head.

"Correction," he said. "*You* have four extra people to worry about."

A hint of a smile crossed his face.

"What are you talking about?" I protested. "I can hardly walk. There's no way I could sneak around to plant your stupid bugs without somebody noticing."

Augustus pulled the car into a space along the street about a half block from the park entrance.

"I said nothing about sneaking," he said. "You simply drop one transmitter on the ground when you reach the reflecting pool. You keep the other one in your shirt pocket in case Previt moves the conversation elsewhere."

He turned off the engine.

"And suppose I'm searched?" I asked.

He reached around to the back seat and drew out the cigar box.

"I doubt Mr. Previt can afford to get that close to you," he said.

Augustus found the two bugs in the box. He put one in my outstretched palm and dropped the other in my shirt pocket.

"Good luck, Michael," Augustus said as I got out of the car with my cane.

I began the slow walk across the Spanish bridge on Laurel Street, which spanned the freeway and led to the center of the park. Sparsely placed streetlamps splashed pockets of yellow light on the handrail.

I feared the night with all its uncertainty. It was not only Previt and Goren I was afraid of. I was an easy target for any thief or derelict who happened to be waiting near the bridge. There was a good reason why Previt had chosen the reflecting pool as our meeting place. No one would be around to bother him. At midnight the park was deserted.

The cane was rubbing a blister on my palm by the time I approached the pool. I whispered quietly into my shirt pocket.

"Augustus, if you can hear me, I'm about fifty yards from the pool. This is the last time I'll be saying anything until Previt gets here."

I limped slowly to the edge of the pool. A single streetlight from across the water reflected among the lily pads. Selecting the darkest spot at the corner of the pool, I opened my left hand and dropped the first bug in the grass. According to my watch it was a minute past midnight. I searched the shadows for Previt.

With each passing minute I grew more and more

anxious. Despite the cool weather my forehead was sweating, and I could feel my heart pounding in my chest. At about twelve-fifteen I thought I heard the snap of a twig in the shadows behind me, but when I turned, I could see nothing, and there was only silence again. Finally, at about twelve-thirty, I saw the dark outline of a man emerging from the shadows. His hand motioned for me to come to the other side of the pool.

One bug left, I thought to myself as I hobbled around the pool, glancing down at the wasted transmitter I had tossed on the ground. The man retreated into the shadows as I approached, so that I could no longer see him by the time I reached the streetlight.

"Over here, Mr. Thompson," a voice beckoned from the darkness. I walked a few steps into the shadows. Suddenly, I recognized the granite features of Charles Previt not six feet away.

"That's far enough," he said. He was holding a pistol.

"Where's Hazel Whittington?" I asked.

His eyes glared. "First things first. Reach into your left front pocket and pull it inside out."

I almost made the mistake of reaching into my shirt pocket. Then I realized he was talking about my pants. I pulled the left front pocket of my jeans inside out.

"Now the right pocket."

I held the cane with my left hand, balancing on one leg as I pulled out my right front pocket.

"Now turn around so I can see your back pockets."

I turned my back toward him.

"You're a smart man," he said. "If you had brought a weapon tonight I might have been tempted to make you use it on Hazel Whittington." The steadiness of his jaw told me he was not bluffing.

"What do you want from me?" I asked, not taking my eyes off his gun.

Previt motioned towards the shadows.

"We're going for a walk," he said. "Just in case you brought your friends."

He gestured again with the pistol.

"You first," he said.

I moved forward into the darkness, staying on the sidewalk as best I could. I could hear Previt's measured footsteps behind me.

"That's far enough," he said when we had left the streetlight far behind. "Don't turn around."

I froze, half expecting to be shot in the back, half waiting for his next instructions. A stiff breeze rustled the leaves around us. I could hear a second pair of footsteps on the grass behind me, then the sound of muffled voices. Then the footsteps went away.

Previt spoke again.

"There's a manila envelope on the sidewalk directly behind you. Pick it up."

I turned and crouched, barely able to see the envelope in the darkness.

"Now walk to the next streetlight."

I carried the manila envelope with my free hand. I stopped when I reached a spot directly under the light.

"There is a legal document inside the envelope. Sign it."

I tore open the envelope and pulled out the document. A ballpoint pen was attached. The caption at the top of the document read, "CONFESSION AND RELEASE FROM LIABILITY." I'd had time enough to skim the first "Whereas" clause when Previt stopped me.

"Sign it!" he ordered.

I continued to read. "This thing says I kidnapped Hazel Whittington," I snapped. "There are witnesses who know I didn't."

"Your witnesses will be taken care of," Previt growled.

I was hoping Augustus was taping all this.

"This document's no good," I said. "No one will believe a lawyer signed a confession just to ease his conscience."

Previt aimed the gun at my face.

"You've got ten seconds to sign," he said.

"All right, all right." I leafed the pages forward to the signature line and signed my full name.

"Let me see it," he ordered, stepping forward quickly to grab the document from my hand.

"Good boy," he said with a smile when he found my signature. "We may be able to work together after all."

He folded the paper and stuffed it inside his coat.

"Where's Hazel Whittington?" I asked again.

Previt gestured with the pistol.

"All in due time," he answered. "Keep walking."

After a few steps we were in darkness again, heading for Park Avenue, on the opposite side of the park from Augustus.

"Stop where you are until that car passes," he said as we approached the end of the sidewalk. The headlights of a car on Park Avenue were visible from about five blocks away. I waited in the shadows until the car passed, then walked down to the curb.

Previt's black Porsche was parked directly in front of me. When I came to within five feet, the passenger door opened and I stood face-to-face with Bob Goren.

"Stop right there," he ordered. I stopped. Goren reached into the car and yanked the seat forward.

"Where's Hazel?" I shouted.

I heard Previt's footsteps behind me.

"That's enough out of you," he spat.

I turned to look at him. As I did, I noticed some movement in the shadows behind Previt. Previt turned a split second after I did.

"Hold it right there!" a voice called from the darkness.

"Get in the car!" Previt yelled, pushing me into the back seat.

Goren jumped into the front seat in front of me. Previt ran around the car to the driver's side. I looked out to where I had seen the movement. Jim Simmons was running toward the car.

"Shut the door!" Previt yelled. Goren slammed it shut. Previt revved the engine and screeched away from the curb.

Bam! Jim fired a warning shot in the air. I ducked below window level. Crash! Another shot blew out the glass quarter panel beside me. Previt accelerated toward the freeway and we were gone—out of gunshot range.

Goren leveled a pistol at me after Previt had pulled onto the freeway.

"Don't try anything stupid," he said.

I kept my thoughts to myself as we drove northward.

When Previt took the freeway exit at Solana Beach I thought he was headed for my condo. Instead, he sped through town and took a narrow country road toward the village of Rancho Santa Fe. About a mile from town he turned left onto a cobblestone driveway and stopped at a set of iron gates. He flashed his lights twice, the gates swung open, and we proceeded down a country lane flanked by heavy foliage and eucalyptus trees. About a mile from the main highway the foliage gave way to a floodlit Georgian mansion. A uniformed security guard met the Porsche when we stopped near the front entrance. He was holding a pair of leashed Dobermans.

"Good evening, Mr. Previt," the guard said, bowing his head to his superior. Previt nodded and got out of the car. Goren opened his door and put one leg out, then turned to face me.

"You will be pleased to learn that I have put my gun away; but, you should know that the guard has orders to loose the dogs on you if you attempt to leave. I would suggest you follow me into the study."

I waited for Goren to crawl out of the front seat, then exited the car myself. The Dobermans snarled and strained at their leashes as I hobbled behind Goren to the front door.

Upon my first step into the mansion, I found myself in a domed foyer flanked by curving marble staircases that met at a balcony on the second floor. Goren led me through a formal parlor, then into a dark library that appeared to double as a study. I recognized a number of the legal reference volumes lining the panels around the desk.

"I was an attorney once myself, you know," Goren remarked when he saw me gazing at the bookshelves.

"No, I didn't know," I replied, and then added with a measure of sarcasm, "Is that where you learned to draft confessions?"

Goren chuckled. Previt entered the library and joined Goren at the desk.

"Please be seated, gentlemen," Goren said. He made a flourish with his fingers. I sat in a leather armchair near the desk.

"I have a business proposition for you, Mr. Thompson."

He turned toward Previt, who handed him the folded document I had signed. I watched as Goren reviewed the document, smiling broadly with an air of pride.

"It's a fine piece of work, if I do say so myself," he said.

"It's worthless trash," I shot back.

Previt and Goren laughed.

"Mr. Thompson doesn't appreciate my work," Goren said. "Maybe I should explain the terms."

Previt chuckled. "An excellent suggestion," he said.

"Please do," I said flatly.

Goren walked around to my side of the desk, waving the document in front of him.

"As you know," he began, "it is quite common for opposite parties in a lawsuit to reach a settlement agreement. Typically, such agreements call for the payment of money by one side and a cessation of hostilities by the other."

"I think I know what a settlement is," I said impatiently.

"Apparently not," Goren continued, "since you have no appreciation for the one you signed."

I glared at Previt, then back at Goren. "I didn't have the pleasure of reading it."

Previt ignored my remark.

"Pity," Goren said. "You might have learned something."

He snapped his fingers loudly.

"Paco!" he called. A white-jacketed servant appeared at the study door. "Please bring a wheelchair for Mr. Thompson. And some coffee for all of us."

The servant bowed his head and disappeared.

Goren continued, "The agreement states that you have committed certain criminal and tortious acts, including illegal entry and invasion of privacy. I am referring of course to your amateurish attempt to bug Mr. Previt's office."

"If you know so much," I said, "you know that a confession obtained under duress is worthless."

Goren shook his head, clicking his teeth.

"Duress? My dear Mr. Thompson. You are a highly valued employee." His words drooled over me like glutinous syrup. "We were shocked to learn that you were engaged in unseemly behavior."

I was not amused. "Finish your story," I said.

Goren smiled. "As you wish. The second half of the document recites what I believe to be your accusations against us, including fraud and embezzlement."

"And kidnapping," I added.

"Let's leave it at fraud and embezzlement," Goren said. He walked back to the other side of the desk. "The document concludes with a paragraph stating that in consideration of one hundred thousand dollars, payable over the course of two years, you have agreed to remain silent about everything concerning your employment at Argotech and to forego any further legal action."

"And what if I refuse the money?" I asked, already knowing the answer.

"Why, we would have no choice but to kill you," Goren said without blinking an eye.

I gulped. "And if I agree to your terms we just go our separate ways?"

Goren nodded. "A simple business proposition."

The servant had returned with a wheelchair, which he positioned next to me. He returned a moment later with cream, sugar, and three mugs of coffee on a tray.

"Of course," Previt added, "we need to ensure that you have deposited and spent the first installment of your money before we can permit you to leave our custody."

The servant handed me a mug of coffee.

"Why is that?" I asked.

Goren answered the question for him. "To ensure that your credibility will be worthless if you ever attempt to challenge us publicly. Once you have spent your new money on a few niceties, it will be easy to prove that your confession was a genuine legal settlement. You can hardly claim duress when you have purchased a new Mercedes with your money."

He pounded his fist on the desk triumphantly.

"But some people might just believe me," I said.

Previt twisted his mustache and laughed.

"No one we'd be worried about," he said. "And besides, you'll enjoy the money."

I started drinking my coffee.

"There is one more item of information we will be needing from you tonight, before we show you to your bedroom," Previt said.

I put the mug down on the arm of the chair.

"What's that?" I asked.

Previt stood up and took one step in my direction.

"You were driven to the park tonight by a man we have never seen before," he continued. "Who was that man?"

I looked from Previt to Goren, unwilling to disclose Augustus's name.

"I didn't get a good look at him," I lied.

Goren stood up next to Previt.

"Come, come, Mr. Thompson," Goren said, "you can do better than that."

I took another swallow of coffee.

"You know his name," I said to Previt. "You called him."

Previt took another step toward me.

"I called Hazel Whittington's son," he said. "The man who drove you to the park was a black man."

I didn't answer. Previt glared at me.

"If we don't find out tonight the easy way, we can find out tomorrow the hard way."

I was going to ask about Hazel when something in the coffee made me too drowsy to speak.

Chapter XIV

I awoke in a Renaissance bedroom. Someone had dressed me in blue silk pajamas and tucked me between the covers of a canopied bed. My clothes were folded on the wheelchair beside me. Looking around the room, I realized with a start that I was not alone. The Mexican servant, dressed in his white jacket and cap, sat by the window, watching me as I stretched.

"Buenos dias, señor," he said. "You wish something for breakfast?"

He stood up and walked to the foot of the bed.

"I wish to go home," I answered gruffly.

The servant shook his head.

"I am sorry, *señor*, but that will not be possible," he said. "*Señor* Goren and *Señor* Previt are waiting for you downstairs. They will be happy to know you are awake."

My stomach felt queasy. The servant moved to the open door like a trained Afghan.

"You will have something for breakfast, no?" he asked again.

"No."

He left the room.

I reached for my clothes on the wheelchair and dressed quickly, looking around for my cane. It was gone. I pulled the wheelchair close to the bed and twisted myself onto the seat. The wheels moved easily as I guided the chair to the door. I could see now that the hallway outside the bedroom was the foyer balcony I had noticed the night before. It was bounded on each end by a marble staircase spiraling down to the front entrance. The giant rotunda loomed above me.

My thoughts were interrupted by the sight of Charles Previt looking up at me from the parlor door.

"Well, look who's wide awake!" he called up to me. "And so early in the afternoon!"

I did not appreciate his sense of humor.

"What did you do with my cane?" I asked.

"Oh, that," Previt said, smiling innocently. "We decided you wouldn't be needing it. Paco is happy to take you anywhere you need to go."

I wheeled myself to the edge of the staircase.

"Tell Paco I'd appreciate it if he would get me down these stairs," I said.

Paco appeared beneath me at the door opposite Previt.

"Be careful, *señor*," he said. "Let me help you."

He bounded up the steps, two at a time.

"Bring him to the back yard," Previt ordered. "We have some unfinished business."

Paco helped me out of the wheelchair.

"You stay here, *señor,* while I carry the wheelchair down the steps."

I held myself steady against the banister. While I was waiting for Paco, I shifted more of my weight to my right ankle to see how much it had healed. I found that it would support me without too much pain. I decided not to share that fact with Previt and Goren. Paco ran up the steps again.

"Lean your weight on me, *señor.*"

He all but carried me down the steps. I sat in the waiting wheelchair and be began pushing me through the parlor to the kitchen. A doorway beside the stove led out to the back yard.

"Ah, good morning, Mr. Thompson," Goren said, when Paco had stopped me on the back lawn.

Goren and Previt were lounging in white wicker chairs. The security guard I had seen the night before was restraining two Dobermans on separate leashes. I could hear more dogs yelping in a wire enclosure at the far end of the lawn.

"You left some questions unanswered," Previt said.

He walked over behind me and guided my wheelchair to within a few feet of the security guard. The dogs were straining to sniff me. Previt withdrew a small vial, like a test tube, from his pocket and poured the contents on my injured ankle.

"This is a wonderful tincture I call 'essence of sirloin'," he said, chuckling. "The dogs are hungry this morning."

The Dobermans could smell the scent. They

lunged and barked. It was all the guard could do to hold them back.

"The man who drove you to the park last night . . . ," Goren prompted. "What was his name?"

I looked away, pretending to be thinking. Previt grabbed one of the leashes from the guard and held the dog within inches of my leg.

"The name, please," he said sternly. The Doberman was straining at the leash and whining.

I hesitated.

"I didn't get a good look at him," I lied.

"Strike!" Previt shouted. The Doberman lunged forward, clamping his teeth on my swollen ankle.

I screamed until my breath gave out. Bursts of pain shot through my tendons like fireworks.

I struggled and kicked, but the hound's teeth clinched tighter. With a sudden lurch I threw myself out of the wheelchair onto the wet grass. The snarling Doberman flipped over beside me without losing its grip. The shredding action of its saberlike teeth was unbearable.

"I'll tell you the name! Get him off!"

I was writhing on the grass, kicking and beating with my left leg and both fists. The dog was too strong for me.

"Back!" Previt commanded.

The Doberman clung to my ankle, but obeyed at last when Previt yanked the leash with both hands. Blood was streaming through my sock to the freshly mown grass. The dog was staring at my leg, drooling hungrily and licking his teeth.

"Quickly!" Previt snapped. "We have no time for games."

My body was numb. I took a deep breath.

"Augustus Martin," I whispered into the grass.

The barking of the Dobermans drowned out my words.

"Louder!" Previt shouted. "What was the name?"

I turned my head toward Previt.

"Augustus Martin," I said in a stronger voice.

"Liar!" Previt screamed, his eyes wide with lunatic rage.

I began to shiver.

"I'm not lying," I pleaded as calmly as I could, my voice shaking. Previt ignored me.

"Paco," he said. "Bring Mrs. Whittington."

Paco disappeared behind the dog cage. He emerged a few seconds later pushing a second wheelchair. Hazel was wearing a gown of blue silk, which matched the material in my pajamas. Her wrists were strapped to the chair arms. When she twisted her face toward mine, I could see that she was gagged. There were tears in her eyes.

My fear became anger. I no longer cared about my ankle, or even about sending Previt to jail. I wanted him dead. I swore to myself that if he let those dogs hurt Hazel, I'd find a way to kill him.

Previt sprinkled drops of liquid from the vial on the exposed portions of her wrists and calves, and set the half-empty bottle on the seat of his wicker chair.

"The other dog!" he ordered.

The security guard came forward with the second Doberman. Previt took the leash and inched both Dobermans toward Hazel's chair.

"Now you will tell us the name, Mr. Thompson."

Previt's eyes were dark. The Dobermans strained against the metal leashes, stretching their collars toward Hazel's legs. She braced herself for the savage attack to follow if I failed to satisfy Previt.

"You've got to believe me," I said, lifting my hands toward Previt in a frantic gesture. "Augustus Martin is Hazel Whittington's adopted son."

Previt's face turned red with fury.

"Strike!" he shouted. Hazel writhed and jerked as the dogs struck her calves, their bloody fangs ripping her flesh again and again. She screamed through her gag.

A high pitched whistle, shrill and loud like feedback from a loudspeaker, stopped the dogs for a moment. The pause was long enough to give me my chance. I lunged toward Previt's wicker chair and grabbed the vial, flinging the liquid on Previt's startled face.

"Strike!" I yelled. My ankle weakened and I fell to the grass again.

The Dobermans sprang for Previt's head. He tumbled to the ground in a fetal position, covering his face with his arms. The Dobermans were all over him, tearing his face into a sickening swirl of dripping tissue and blood. Although he thrashed and kicked, Previt could not cry out, for the front of his throat had been ripped away in one piece by the larger dog, the one now ripping feverishly at Previt's ear.

It may have been the nauseous, gurgling sound emerging from Previt's freshly exposed voicebox that lifted me to my knees. I remember emptying my stomach in a series of convulsive heaves before I passed out.

When I opened my eyes, Jim Simmons was running into the back yard, his pistol drawn. The detective was right behind him.

"Call off the dogs!" Jim ordered.

Paco and the security guard had already grabbed the leashes and were pulling the dogs away from Previt's mangled face. I looked back at Hazel. Her clothes were spattered with blood.

"Now up against the fence." Jim forced Goren into a spread-eagle position. The detective trained a pistol on Paco and the guard as they returned the dogs to the cage. He pulled a walkie-talkie from his coat.

"We've got two for the hospital," he said.

A team of medics came running around the corner of the mansion and laid stretchers in front of us. My mind was fading in and out of consciousness—more from the shock of what I had seen than from the extent of my own injuries. I was unaware of being carried to the front driveway, but I can remember Sheila's freckled face staring down at me when they set me on the grass next to the ambulance.

"I told you you'd be glad you hired me," she said, grinning. She leaned over and gave me a gentle hug.

"But you were dead," I answered. I was too bewildered to squeeze back.

"Wrong, airhead," she laughed.

My fear returned suddenly as Goren appeared at the corner of the building. Then I saw that the detective was marching behind him with a pistol.

He stopped when he saw me lying on the stretcher. "I know where to find you when I get out," he said.

I pretended to ignore the comment. Instead, I spoke to Sheila in a voice loud enough for Goren to hear.

"How long do you suppose he'll be in for?" I asked, winking at Sheila.

She played along.

"Let's see," she began in a stage voice, as if the world were listening. "He's facing thirty-to-life on two counts of kidnapping, fifteen years for the burglary at your condo, twenty years each on two counts of attempted murder, and about ten to twenty more for assorted felonies."

I raised up and nodded to Goren.

"Let me know if you need someone to take care of your dogs while you're away," I said, and laid my head back down on the stretcher.

The medics had loaded Hazel into the ambulance. Then they reached down and hoisted me inside. Sheila and Augustus climbed in beside me.

"Augustus!" I wheezed when I saw him.

He patted me on the shoulder and found a place next to Hazel.

"I know I'm a little foggy," I said, as the ambulance rumbled down the cobblestone driveway, "but I could have sworn I heard feedback from a loudspeaker back there. What was that noise?"

Sheila winked at Augustus and began massaging the sides of my neck.

"That was an electronic dog whistle," she said. "Your friend, Augustus, has a way with sound equipment."

I don't remember the rest of the trip.

When I opened my eyes I was lying on my back in a narrow hospital bed. The huge figure of Augustus Martin towered over me.

"How do you feel?" he asked.

My right ankle felt like an overstuffed pin cushion.

"Oh, wonderful," I answered. "I love doggies."

Augustus laughed. "Sorry," he said. "Our timing was a little off."

I pulled myself up into a sitting position and looked around.

"How's Hazel?" I asked.

Augustus sat on the bed beside me.

"I took her home," he replied. "They treated her leg and released her. The two of you had similar wounds—multiple bites and muscle tears—but Mum never lost consciousness. No offense, but I think she's bearing up better than you."

I smiled at the news. "I think we may have underestimated her," I said.

Augustus nodded. "She's a tough bird all right." He pushed the nurse's call button on my nightstand.

"You mind telling me what happened back there?" I asked.

Augustus scratched his chin smugly and walked over to the window.

"You might have to wait a few hours for that. Sheila made me promise not to tell you anything until she could join us for champagne."

He walked back to the bed.

"Excellent," I said. "I get to drink champagne with a dead woman."

Augustus gave me one of his toothy grins.

"Chin up, old boy," he said. "The nurse told me you were free to leave when you woke up. Despite my lack of medical training, I would hazard a guess that you are no longer asleep."

A heavyset nurse walked into the room.

"Awake, I see," she said.

She marched straight at me and shoved an electronic thermometer in my mouth.

"We have his cane at the nurses' station," she said to Augustus. "His clothes are in the closet behind the bed."

Augustus opened the closet door behind me. He rustled around for a few moments and handed me my clothes. There were no bloodstains on the trousers.

"Where did this pair come from?" I asked, as the nurse removed the thermometer.

Augustus gave me a hand as I twisted my body around to the edge of the bed.

"I sent Penny to fetch them from your suitcase," he said. "The detective wanted to save the bloodstained pair for the jury."

I slid the right trouser leg gingerly over my bandaged ankle.

"Oh, yes," Augustus said. "I almost forgot. We shall all be meeting at my house tonight. We thought you might have a few questions to ask."

"A minor understatement," I said, buckling my belt.

Epilogue

It was after dark when Augustus drove me back to North Park. My ankle was still swollen from the bites, but I was able to limp behind him without any help. When we entered the living room, I was surprised to find a half-dozen faces waiting to greet us. Penny and the detective were seated on the love seat. Sheila was by herself on the sofa. A man I had never seen before sat in the armchair to her left. He was holding a small boy in his lap. A champagne bottle rested in an ice bucket on the coffee table. Without a word to anyone, Augustus hurried back to Hazel's bedroom.

I must have begun staring at the detective, because he stood and introduced himself. "I'm Joe Boykins, Penny and Sheila's father." He walked toward me, extending his hand.

My jaw dropped. Sheila laughed and pulled me down next to her before I could move a muscle. I managed a halfhearted handshake, and Joe Boykins returned to the love seat. Everyone smiled but me.

Augustus returned a moment later. From the grin on his face I knew Hazel was all right. He pulled the dripping bottle out of the ice bucket, unwrapped the neck, and popped the cork. Everyone cheered and clapped. He passed champagne glasses around the room.

"I propose a toast," he began. The group hushed. "To the man who got us all into this mess."

I was a little slow on the uptake. "You mean Charles Previt?" I asked.

Sheila elbowed me. "He means you, airhead." Everyone howled.

Augustus poured the champagne and seven people attempted to clink glasses with every other person. Even Penny and the boy got a taste.

When we had settled back in our seats Sheila poked me in the ribs. "Any questions?" She winked at the others.

I shook my head. "Aside from your rising from the dead and our being kidnapped by your father, everything makes perfect sense."

Everybody laughed again.

"Let's start with me," she said. "What do you want to know?"

I cleared my throat. "Well, for starters, I thought your Fiat went through the railing on the Ingraham Street Bridge."

She patted my hand affectionately. "Let's start with the accident. You remember I copied down that Gopher address from the letter you showed me in my office? Well, after we left Nolan's, I drove to Crown Point. When I got there, the mailman was sorting the mail. I told him I was Terrell's wife. He found a letter for James Terrell and gave it to me. It was the same as the one you showed me."

"The same letter?" I asked.

"Identical," she said. "Previt caught me reading it and chased me in his Porsche."

I nodded. "We saw the tire tracks."

Sheila's face showed traces of the horror she had experienced during that chase.

"It was all I could do to stay in front of him. But he caught me on the bridge. I tried to lose him but his Porsche was too quick. He swerved into me and knocked my car into the other lanes."

"Toward the oncoming traffic?" I asked.

She squeezed my fingers. "Right. Luckily no one was coming the other way. I was really hitting the brakes hard. I thought I'd stopped by the time I hit the railing. In fact, the tires caught one of the girders on the bridge, so I was just seesawing over the edge. I don't know how I escaped. I just jumped out—God, I was falling."

"Whew!" I whistled. "You dove from a hundred feet? You're lucky to be alive."

"It was only about fifty feet," she said, "and I went in feetfirst. I don't remember anything after that, except waking up in a rowboat."

The young boy chimed in. "I saw you first, didn't I!"

Sheila laughed. "You sure did. Michael, this is Pete Sargent and his father, Ned. They saved my life."

I nodded to Ned and Pete.

"Daddy didn't want to go," Pete said, "but I made him."

His father smiled. "That's right. Wasn't sure I wanted Pete to see that kind of thing. Thought she was drowned for sure, and damned if the car didn't fall right in behind her. Missed her by maybe five feet. Suction pulled her under again. Shocked the hell out of me when we fished her out and she starts breathing and talking. First thing she does is make us all promise not to tell no one about the accident. Wanted to take her to the hospital and she wouldn't even let me do *that*."

"So, Ned drove me home." Sheila drained the last few drops from her champagne glass. "I got some clothes together and he took me to Dad's house. That's when Dad assured him the police would handle everything."

I was more confused now than when she had started.

"But I went to your funeral," I said.

That remark brought a loud giggle from Penny. "You went to her memorial service," she blurted. "Remember seeing a coffin?"

Sheila squeezed my hand. "I kept worrying that you'd start asking questions around the morgue, so I called Jim. That's when he entered the picture."

I looked around the room. "Where is he, anyway?"

Sheila grinned. "Home with his wife. She blew a fuse when she found out he was helping me. Can't say as I blame her. I'm better looking than she is."

Penny stuck a finger down her throat and made a gagging noise.

"So what was Jim supposed to do at the morgue?" I asked.

"I told him to keep you out of there," Sheila answered.

"But you never came near the place," Penny chirped.

Sheila poked me again in my sore ribs. "We must have overestimated your intelligence."

I looked at Penny. "So why didn't you tell us Sheila was alive? It might have saved Hazel and me from having to do our dog food imitation."

Penny straightened up proudly. "Sheila wanted to conduct her own investigation without anyone knowing she was alive. Jim and I were supposed to report back to Sheila about everything you guys were doing. We also had to make sure you didn't get in the way too much."

"Thanks a lot," I said, sticking out my tongue at her.

Sheila's father pointed at me. "You know good and well you would've gone straight to Sheila if you'd known she survived the crash. Previt was following you everywhere you went. He would've seen her alive and he'd have gone after her again."

I paused to collect my thoughts. "But why were you working against us? Why didn't you and Jim stop the police from arresting us as Argotech?"

He pulled a slip of paper from his pocket. "The security guard wrote down your license plate and description the first night you guys showed up there. He thought you looked suspicious."

Augustus chuckled at that.

Boykins continued. "The guard gave your license number and description to his supervisor the next day, and the supervisor showed Previt. Previt called a friend of his in the Department of Motor Vehicles and got Hazel's address." He stuffed the paper back in his pocket.

"But that doesn't answer why the police picked us up," I said.

Boykins shook his head. "We didn't want to raise Previt's suspicions. Once he tipped us off that you might be coming, we had to show up to make it look good. It was bad enough that Jim talked me into letting you out of jail. Previt was on TV the next day giving us hell for that."

I was still trying to fit all the pieces together in my mind. "So why didn't Previt hang around here and get us?"

Augustus spoke up. "That's exactly what Previt did. But when he got here you and I had gone over to Argotech again. Mum didn't have any idea where we were, so she couldn't answer his questions. Previt decided to use her for bait."

I looked at Joe Boykins.

"So why'd you kidnap us at the beach, right when we were starting to tape Previt and Goren?"

Boykins leaned forward. "I had no way of knowing what you were doing. I thought you were screwing up our investigation. As it turned out,

Augustus captured enough admissions on those beach tapes to put Goren and Previt away for life."

I thought back to the Holiday Inn. "Were the handcuffs really necessary?"

Boykins smiled sheepishly. "It was the only way I could protect you boys. If you'd stayed in the hotel where I left you, we'd have arrested Goren and Previt in Balboa Park."

"But if anything had gone wrong they'd have killed Hazel," I said.

Boykins nodded. "I'm glad everything turned out the way it did."

"So why didn't you move in when you saw Goren and Previt push me into the Porsche? I saw Jim firing his pistol at the car, but I didn't see you."

Boykins smiled. "Jim was a little restless with that pistol. I didn't want to risk hitting you with a stray bullet."

I was starting to understand. "Just one more question. What was the deal about those letters? Why did Previt write two letters to himself?"

Augustus cleared his throat, "I believe I can answer that one. The weak link in Previt's chain turned out to be Lisa Crenshaw, his secretary. You will recall how helpful Lisa was in guiding us to the Cardiff Fish House. Previt was afraid to include her in his conspiracy."

"But what has that got to do with the letters?" I asked.

Augustus sighed. "You barristers are always missing the forest for the trees. Previt needed a neutral witness in case the company auditors questioned the payments. Lisa could have supplied them with a file copy of the letter, and the payments would not have been questioned. No one would have doubted the existence of Gopher, Inc., because she would have sworn on a stack of Bibles that she mailed the letter out herself."

"But why the second letter?" I persisted.

"Lisa was the one who typed the letter you intercepted on Thursday afternoon. Having lost the first one, she simply typed another one and mailed it out. Previt was not aware that two copies existed until Lisa told him the next day."

I chuckled to myself. "I'm surprised we didn't think of that earlier."

Augustus nodded. "Quite."

Ned stood up and motioned to his son. "Pete and I have to be going. It was a pleasure meeting you."

He shook my hand and turned to leave. Joe Boykins waved to everyone and followed Ned to the door. Penny danced over and planted a wet kiss on my forehead. I remembered how she looked in the blonde wig.

"Next time I need a good disguise I'll look you up," I said.

She made a face. "You might just need a disguise. I think my sister likes you."

Augustus burst out laughing. Penny turned and ran toward the front door. Sheila pulled her hand quickly from mine and rose up as if to chase her sister.

"Brat," she muttered.

"I think it's time we visited Hazel," I said to Augustus when the three of us were alone.

We went back to Hazel's bedroom and found her lying on top of the sheet with no bedspread. Her arms and legs were spangled with bandages. I had expected to find Spike on the bed with her, but there was no cat in sight.

"Where's my cat?" I asked as I leaned over to give Hazel a gentle hug.

"Didn't Augustus tell you?" she said. "He took Spike back home for you after he brought me home. He had to unlock your door for the housecleaners anyway."

"He did what?" I asked incredulously.

"The keys were in your pants pocket at the hospital," Augustus said. "We hired a cleaning service to do the rest. We did not think it proper that you return to a ransacked condominium."

I was too stunned to speak.

"Mum, you remember Sheila," Augustus said.

Sheila smiled at Hazel.

"Yes, of course," Hazel said. "We met in the hospital."

I thought of all the help Augustus and Hazel had given me, and of the death of Tigger and Jinx. I felt very solemn.

"I never should have brought all this trouble to your house."

Hazel slapped me playfully on the hand. "Nonsense," she said. "It's all over now. You should have come to us for help much sooner than you did."

My eyes were starting to water. Augustus noticed and changed the subject.

"What will you be doing now?" he asked. "I mean about your job and all. You won't be going back to Argotech, will you?"

I laughed between sniffles. "Hardly. You know, I haven't even thought about any of that."

Sheila linked her arm in mine.

"I thought I might discuss a business proposition with him this evening," she said to Augustus and Hazel. "That is, if he'll let me cook dinner at his place."

She gave them a wink.

"Tell her I'm not used to having dinner with dead people," I said, "but I'll try it just this once."

Augustus and Hazel laughed.

I shook Augustus's hand warmly as we walked to the front door. "Thanks for everything."

He pounded me on the back with his free hand. "Hopefully it won't be fifteen years before I see you again."

"No way."

Sheila explained her business plans as she drove me to the condo.

"We're already getting a lot of new business from the publicity on this thing," she began. "Dad's thinking about retiring and joining me. I know it's kind of crazy sounding, but have you ever thought of becoming a private investigator?"

For some reason the question didn't sound crazy to me at all. "Funny you should ask," I said. "For a while there, I almost enjoyed all the excitement."

I gestured at the Solana Beach exit sign.

"Well, think it over," she said. "It'll be a family business, but you're more than welcome to join."

She stopped at the traffic light at the end of the exit ramp.

"Join the family?" I joked

The light turned green.

"No. The business." She blushed. The tires squealed as we left the intersection.

The evening sun was melting into the water by the time we reached the stairway outside my condo. Sheila held my cane and I grabbed the banister to pull myself up the steps. I had also handed her the front door key, but she waited for me at the landing before she turned the key in the lock.

I was adjusting the cane in my hand when I saw it coming. Sheila screamed before I could stop the white streak from falling on her neck.

"Dammit, Spike!" I yelled.

FREE!!
BOOKS BY MAIL
CATALOGUE

BOOKS BY MAIL will share with you our current bestselling books as well as hard to find specialty titles in areas that will match your interests. You will be updated on what's new in books at no cost to you. Just fill in the coupon below and discover the convenience of having books delivered to your home.

PLEASE ADD $1.00 TO COVER THE COST OF POSTAGE & HANDLING.

BOOKS BY MAIL

320 Steelcase Road E.,   210 5th Ave., 7th Floor
Markham, Ontario L3R 2M1   New York, N.Y., 10010

Please send Books By Mail catalogue to:

Name _____
(please print)

Address _____

City _____

Prov./State _____ P.C./Zip _____
(BBM1)